D1234430

THE PRINCE'S
CAPTIVE VIRGIN

THE PRINCE'S CAPTIVE VIRGIN

BY

MAISEY YATES

First published in Great Britain 2017
By Mills & Boon, an imprint of HarperCollins*Publishers*
1 London Bridge Street, London, SE1 9GF

Large Print edition 2017

© 2017 Maisey Yates

ISBN: 978-0-263-07143-6

Printed and bound in Great Britain
by CPI Antony Rowe, Chippenham, Wiltshire

To my dad.

Remember when you took me to see
Beauty and the Beast when I was seven?

I think all of this is your fault.
And I love you.

CHAPTER ONE

Once upon a time...

BELLE LOOKED UP at the imposing castle and tightened her coat more firmly around her petite frame. It was surprisingly chilly tonight on the small island country nestled in the Aegean Sea between Greece and Turkey.

Of course, when she had first heard of Olympios she had been put in mind of the Mediterranean. Bright white homes and searing blue skies and seas. And perhaps, in the daytime, that was what it was. But here at night, with the velvet darkness settled low around her and that damp air blowing in from the ocean, it felt like something completely unexpected.

The fortress in front of her, on the other hand, was almost far too expected. It was medieval, and nothing but the lights flickering in the window gave any indication that it might be part of the modern era. Of course, she could expect nothing less from a man who had gone to such great lengths to seek revenge on a photographer.

A man who had captured her father in the act of taking pictures and imprisoned him to get revenge for something as innocuous as photographs that were set to be published without his permission.

Belle supposed that she should be afraid. After all, Prince Adam Katsaros had proven to be unreasonable. He had proven to be inhumane. But she was bolstered by the same rage that had infused her veins from the moment she had first heard of her father's fate, even now.

It seemed that she was insulated from fear, which was strange considering she'd spent a lot of her life feeling afraid of almost everything. Of losing her father and the haven she'd found with him after her mother had abandoned her when she was four years old. Of the potential inside herself to become a tempestuous, selfish creature driven by passions of the flesh, as her mother had been and probably still was.

All that fear was gone now. Had been from the moment she had first boarded her plane in LA, all the way through her layover in Greece, and through the flight that carried her here to Olympios.

She could only hope that her bravado lasted.

Tony was going to be so mad when he found out she'd done this. Her boyfriend of nearly eight months had always wanted to be more involved in her life. But she resisted. Just like she'd been resisting serious physical intimacy. That was part of all her fear stuff.

She'd never had a boyfriend before, and she was accustomed to her space and her independence. Surrendering any of it just didn't sit well with her.

Which was an ironic thought, considering what she was prepared to do here today.

She was surprised to find that the palace was more or less unguarded. There was no one about as she walked up the steps that led to a rough-hewn double door. She was tempted—not for the first time since her arrival on the island—to check and see if her phone calendar had been set back into the last century. Or, perhaps, a few centuries ago.

She lifted her hand, unsure as to whether or not one knocked on doors like this. In the end, she decided to grasp hold of the iron ring and pull it open. It creaked and groaned with the effort, as though no one had dared enter the large, imposing building in quite some time. However, she knew that they had. Because only a few days ago her father had been brought here. And—if rumor was to be believed—he was being imprisoned on the property.

She took a cautious step inside, surprised by the warmth that greeted her. It was dark, except for some wall sconces that were lit across the room. The great stone antechamber possessed nothing like the sort of comforts she would have expected from a palace. Not that she was in the habit of being admitted into palaces.

No, the little seaside home she and her father lived in in Southern California was as far from a palace as it was possible to get. It wasn't even Rodeo Drive.

But this wasn't exactly what she had expected

from royalty. In spite of her lack of experience, she did have expectations. She might never have been admitted into the lavish homes and parties that celebrities threw in Beverly Hills, but her father's business was photographing those events. So she had a visual familiarity with them, even if it wasn't based in experience.

"Hello?" she called out into the dim chamber, vaguely aware that that might not have been the best idea the moment the word left her mouth and ricocheted off the stone walls. But, that adrenaline that had wrapped itself around her like an impenetrable suit of armor remained. She had a mission, and she was not going to be frightened out of carrying it out.

Once the prince understood, he would be more than happy to return her father to her custody. She was certain. Once he understood about her father's health.

"Hello?" she called again. Still nothing.

She heard a soft sound, footsteps on the flagstone floor, and she turned toward a corridor that was at the far left of the room, just in time to see a tall, slender man walking toward her. "Are you lost, *kyria*?"

His tone was soft and kind, faintly accented and nothing like the harsh, brutal surroundings that she found herself in. Nothing at all like she had imagined finding here in this medieval keep.

"No," she said, "I'm not lost. My name is Belle Chamberlain and I looking for my father. Mark Chamberlain. He's being held here by the Prince…and I… I don't think he understands."

The servant—at least, that's what she assumed he was—took a step closer to her, his expression becoming clearer as he moved nearer. He looked…concerned. "Yes. I know about that. It is, perhaps, best if you go, Kyria Chamberlain."

"No. You don't understand. My father is ill, and he was supposed to start treatment back home in the States. He can't be here. He can't be…imprisoned, just because he took some photographs that the Prince doesn't like."

"There is a lot here that protects the Prince's privacy," the man said, as though she hadn't spoken. As though he were simply reciting from a well-memorized book. "And whatever the Prince says is…well, it is law."

"I'm not leaving without my father. I'm not leaving until I speak to the Prince. Also, your security is shockingly lax." She looked around. "Nobody stopped me from entering. I imagine it was far too easy for my father to gain access to him. If he wants to keep his life private, then he should work harder at it." The celebrities her father photographed went to great lengths to avoid his telephoto lens. She was not impressed with the setup the Prince had here.

Perhaps it was a little bit callous of her to look at things that way. But, she had been raised the daughter of a paparazzo, and that was just the way things were. Celebrities capitalized on their images, and relied on the fact that they were public commodities. Her father was simply a part of that economy.

"Believe me," the man said. "You don't want to speak to the Prince."

She drew up to her full height, which, admittedly at five-three was not terribly impressive. "Believe me," she countered. "I most certainly do want to speak to the Prince. I want to tell him that his tyrannical tactics, seizing an American citizen, all in the name of his precious vanity, are not the least bit impressive to me. In fact, if he has issues with his presumably weak chin, subtly rounded jawline and hollow chest, perhaps he could take some of the money he has saved by not renovating this palace and invest in a good plastic surgeon, rather than imprisoning a man for taking a few photographs."

"Weak chin?" Another voice sounded in the darkness. Much different from the voice of the servant. It was deep; it resonated there in the stone room, resonated inside Belle. And then, for the first time, she knew fear. An intense, trembling kind that skated down her spine and reverberated in her stomach. "That is a new accusation, I have to say. However, suggestions that I go visit a plastic surgeon are not. I find that I have lost patience with going under the knife, though."

"Prince Adam," the servant said, his tone clearly intended to placate.

"You may leave us, Fos."

"But, Your Majesty—"

"Don't bow and scrape," the Prince said, his tone hard as the stone walls all around them. "It is embarrassing. For you."

"Yes," the man said, "of course."

And then, the one person who she felt might be her ally shuffled back off into the darkness. And she was left with a disembodied voice that was still shrouded in the inky blackness.

"So," he said, "you have come to see about your father."

"Yes," she said, her tone unsteady. She took a deep breath, tried to get a grip on herself. She was not easily intimidated. She never had been. She had spent her childhood going to private schools that she was far too poor to have gained admittance to, if not for a trust fund previously established by her long-deceased grandfather.

Everyone there knew she was there on charity, and she had been forced to grow a spine early. Everyone was always teasing her. For being poor. For always having her head in the clouds—well, she had her nose firmly planted in a book. But, those stories, those fictional worlds, were her armor. They allowed her to insulate herself.

Allowed her to ignore the taunting happening around her.

She had survived a childhood surrounded by the mocking glances and cruel words of the children of Hollywood royalty. Surely she could face down the Prince of a country that was the size of a postage stamp.

She heard a heavy footfall, an indication that he had moved deeper into the room, but she still couldn't see him. "I arrested your father," he said.

"I know that," she said, doing her best to keep her tone steady. "And I think it was a mistake."

He chuckled, but there was no humor in the sound. It lay flat in the room, making it feel as though the temperature had dropped. "You're either very brave or very stupid. Coming to my country, my home, and insulting me."

"I'm not sure that I'm either. I'm just a girl who's concerned about her father. Surely you can understand that."

"Perhaps," he returned. "Though, I find it difficult to remember. I have not worried about my father in quite some time. The cemetery keeps him in good comfort."

She wasn't sure what she was supposed to say to that. If she was supposed to say that she was sorry that his father was dead. In the end, she imagined that he probably didn't want her sympathy.

"That's what I'm afraid will happen to my father," she said. "He's sick. He needs treatment. That was why he got the pictures of you in the first place. He needed money to cover the cost of the treatment that the insurance wouldn't. This is his job. He's a photographer. He's—"

"I have absolutely no interest in paparazzi scum. That kind of thing is forbidden in my country."

"No freedom of the press, then," she said, crossing her arms and planting her feet more firmly against the stone floor.

"No freedom to hunt people down as though they are animals simply because you wish to collect photographs."

She huffed. "I doubt you were hunted down. I was able to gain admittance to the palace easily enough. My father is an experienced photographer, and I bet it was even easier for him."

"He was also caught. Unfortunately, he had also already sent the photographs off to his boss in the United States. And, as his boss is unwilling to negotiate with me—"

"I know. The photographs are planned to go out in an exclusive later this week. I spoke to the *Daily Star.*"

"But they are so invested in the fact my interim leader's tenure has now come up, they want the monopoly on these photographs for when I make my decision about my rule."

"If I *had* been able to negotiate with them," Belle continued, "I wouldn't have come myself. But, I imagined that they didn't explain to you about my father's illness."

"Am I supposed to care? He does not care about *my* afflictions."

Rage poured through her. "Are your afflictions going to kill you? Because his will. If he doesn't get back to the US and get himself into treatment, he is going to die. And I won't let that happen. I can't. You want him sitting here wasting away in a jail cell? For what? Your pride? He can be of no use to you."

She heard him as he began to pace, his footsteps echoing off the walls. She could just make out a dark shape, movement. He was large, but that was all she could gather.

"Perhaps you have a point. Perhaps he is of no use to me. Beyond the fact that I feel the need to make him an example."

"An example to who?"

"Anyone who might dare to do similar. Is it not enough, what was done to my family already? The press feel the need to come back and add insult to injury near the third anniversary of the accident? I will not allow it."

"So, you'll let a dying man rot away in your palace then. Haven't you ever heard that two wrongs don't make a right?"

"You mistake me," he said, his tone suddenly fierce. "I am not trying to make anything right. What has been done to me can never be made right. I want a pound of flesh."

She heard his footsteps, and, she realized, he had turned away from her. That he was beginning to walk away. "No!"

"I am finished with you," he said. "My servant will show you out."

"Take me." The words left her trembling lips before she had a chance to think them through. "Instead of my father. Let me take his place."

"Why would you want to do that?" She heard his footsteps drawing nearer to her again. She blinked hard, cursing her inability to see through the thick darkness.

"*Want* is a strong word. But, I'm not currently in need of medical treatment. If I stay here in your palace for however long the sentence might be… I'll be fine." There was the matter of her scholarship, of the fact that she was supposed to be getting her master's in literature. But, for her father's life, she would easily sacrifice a piece of paper.

"And what good will that do?"

"Just tell everybody that I'm the one who took the pictures. That I am the one who caused all this trouble. Use me as your example." He said nothing. It was so still and silent in the room that she thought he might have left. "Please."

"If we do this, I am not simply letting you off with such a bland public story. No."

"I thought you wanted to make an example of him."

"I did," he said, his tone hard. "However… I think there are more creative uses for you."

A shiver ran through her. Fear. "I don't think you want me for…for that."

"You mistake me. If I wanted a whore, I could have one summoned easily enough. You…you're beautiful. Uncommonly so. And I find myself in an interesting position."

"What?"

"Your father didn't decide to get my photograph on a whim. In the last three years, an interim ruler has been governing in my stead. But that… that period has ended. His term has ended. And I have a choice to make. Whether or not I abdicate for good, or take control of what is mine."

The air rushed from her lungs, a strange metallic taste on her tongue. "And…and you've decided?"

"I will not hide away forever," he said. "I will reclaim my throne. And in that I will make my example. I and my country will not remain broken. And I will not be kept under siege by the press."

"Well I… I don't know anything about ruling a country. I can't help you with that."

"Silly girl. I don't need your brain. I need what I myself no longer possess. I need your beauty."

She could scarcely understand the words he was saying.

"So, you have a deal," he said.

He'd given her no time to react to his previous statement. The swift proclamation stunned her. She nearly stumbled, nearly fell down to her knees.

"I… I do?" She still wasn't sure what she'd agreed to. Helping him somehow with this reclamation of his kingdom. But she had no clue what that actually meant.

"Of course. I will have Fos go and tell your father that he's free to go."

"I…" She didn't know what to say. She certainly didn't feel anything like triumph. Instead, she was terrified, a bitter cold spreading through her midsection. She was a prisoner now. She had agreed to take her father's place in this madman's castle. "Can I…can I see him before he goes?"

"No," he said, "that would only cause unnecessary tears. And I find myself low on patience this evening."

"I don't…what do you want me to do?"

"You have heard it said, I imagine, that behind every successful man is a woman? You will be that woman. Something to help soften my… image."

He turned away again, his footsteps indicating that he was walking away, and panic gripped her. "Wait!"

He stopped. "A servant will come and show you to your room."

She imagined by "room" he meant "dungeon." Another shiver wound through her, fear spiking her blood, making her feel like she had been drugged. "At least let me see you." She refused to think of him as a monster looming around in the darkness. That would only give him more power. He was just a man. As she had been ranting earlier, he was probably a man with a weak chin.

A man who was afraid to show himself because

he was cowardly. Because he was the kind of tyrant who wouldn't allow anyone to say anything about him that wasn't expressly approved by him. She had nothing to fear from this man. And when she saw his face, she would know that for sure.

"If you insist." Footsteps moved toward her, and his shape became clearer as he drew closer. Then one foot moved into the pool of light at the center of the room. Followed by the rest of him.

She had been right in her assessment of him as large. He was almost monstrous in stature, broad and impossibly tall. But if his height weren't enough to make her shiver in fear, his face would have accomplished it.

She had been wrong. He did not have a weak chin. Neither did he have a rounded jaw. No, there was something utterly perfect about his bone structure, which made the damage done to his features seem like a blasphemy shouted in a church.

His skin was golden brown, and it was ruined. Deep grooves taken from his face, a deep slash cutting through one eye. Deep enough that she wondered if he had vision on the side. He might have smiled, but it was difficult to say. The scar tissue at his mouth, so heavy on the one side, kept his lips from tipping up fully.

In that moment, she was certain that she had not been taken captive by a man. No, she had been taken captive by a beast.

CHAPTER TWO

PRINCE ADAM KATSAROS was no longer a handsome man. The accident that had stolen his wife from him had also stolen his face. But, he found it of little concern. He was not a good man anymore, either. And that made it seem slightly more poetic, his outsides matching what remained within.

Though, taking a woman captive was a bit much, even for him. Still, he was not inclined to change his mind now. When she had put the offer on the table, he had accepted it gladly. Mostly because he knew that he could use her. That he would be able to use her much more sufficiently than her father.

If what she said was true, if the old man was in fact dying, he had no interest in keeping him here to do just that. Yes, he wanted to make him an example. Yes, he wanted to reinforce his power, his hard line that he drew against all forms of entertainment media and the low, crawling worms who harassed and tormented their subjects simply for being famous, for being royal.

But, he had no interest in causing anyone's death. Additionally, he had a feeling that this woman could be infinitely more useful. His seclusion was coming to an end, and while he would happily stay in the darkness forever, it could not be so.

The agreement he had signed with the viceroy had very definitive terms. And if Adam didn't step in, an election would take place in the fall. So would go his bloodline, which had ruled Olympios for hundreds of years.

And, lost in his grief and pain though he'd been, he was not so lost that he would abandon all that his family line had built over the centuries.

But he needed another headline. One that extended beyond his scars, and a beautiful woman coming into public view by his side would add another dimension, another story, to the mix.

It was exactly what he needed, though he had not known it.

He would simply need the proper venue in which to use her.

He curled his hand into a fist and looked down at his marred skin. Sometimes, he was tempted to ask himself if he was overreacting. But then he was reminded. It was easy to be reminded. The reminders were all over his body.

At that moment, his phone rang, and he cursed. Because it was his friend—if that was the appropriate word—Prince Felipe Carrión de la Viña Cortez.

He punched the answer button on the phone and lifted it to his ear. "What do you want, Felipe?"

"And hello to you too," came his friend's lazy response. "I have Rafe on the line, as well, just so you know."

"A conference call?" Adam asked. "What sort of trouble are you in?"

His hot-blooded friend had a reputation for causing international incidents, and it wouldn't surprise Adam if he was involved in yet another scandal.

Truly, he, Felipe and Rafe could not be more

different. Were it not for their friendships formed at a particularly strict boarding school, he doubted they would have two words to say to each other now.

But, Felipe and Rafe had kept him from receding completely into darkness over the past few years. And for that, he owed them. Or, at least, for that he didn't growl at them every time one of them made contact.

"No trouble," Felipe said. "However, I am planning a party. You see, it is the fiftieth anniversary of my father's rule. And, likely the last he will see. Of course, I should like to invite you both."

For the first time since getting on the line, Rafe spoke. "And are you allowing service animals at your event?"

Felipe laughed. "Perhaps, Rafe, it is time you found yourself a lovely partner to help lead you around."

"As appealing as that is, I have yet to find a woman keen on playing the part of guide dog."

Five years earlier Rafe had been blinded in an accident, and though Adam didn't know the details, he suspected that a woman had been involved somehow. But, Rafe wasn't the type to share the details of his life. Unlike Felipe and himself, Rafe was not royalty. He had not been born with money. Instead, he had become the protégé of an Italian businessman at a very young age.

That man had paid for Rafe's schooling, and had gotten him a position at his company. Until Rafe's accident. But, it was that accident that had propelled Rafe to the next level of his success. Now he was unquestionably one of the wealthiest and most powerful men in Europe—royal blood or not.

But, whatever had happened, his friend had been completely changed by it. Adam understood.

Growing up, he and Felipe had been hellions. Utterly unconcerned with the state of their education, where Rafe had taken everything seriously. He had been there on borrowed money, and he had been incredibly conscious of that.

Adam and Felipe had spent most of their time pursuing women; Rafe had studied.

Now here they were. All a bit battle worn, except perhaps Felipe. Though, Adam always wondered about his seemingly carefree friend. In his experience, few people were actually carefree, and those that seemed the most dedicated to such facades often had the most structural damage beneath the surface.

"Now," Felipe said, "I'm sure that isn't true. Once a woman gets a look at the size of your... bank account, certainly she's more than willing to fulfill whatever duties you might require."

"Your confidence in me is astounding," Rafe said.

"Well," he continued, "you certainly possess more charm than our friend Adam."

Adam gritted his teeth. "Regretfully, I doubt I will be able to attend your ball."

"That," Felipe said, "is expected. But unacceptable. The fact of the matter is I'm going to be ascending the throne of my country soon. My father might have walled us off, made us insular, but I don't intend to keep it that way. I want to align myself with you, Adam, with your country, and with you, Rafe, and the industry that you could bring to Santa Milagro.

"I know you have been in exile for the past few years, Adam, but with your viceroy's tenure coming to an end, and the recent sale of those photographs of yours to the tabloids, I think it's time you took matters into your own hands. Your visage—such as it is—is going to filter out into the public soon enough. You might as well make an appearance along with it, Adam. Prove that you are not a coward."

"I'm not," he said, quickly losing patience with Felipe. "However, exposing myself in the public arena holds no appeal."

"Certainly understandable. I'm sure if Rafe could hide away, he would do so, as well."

Rafe laughed, but the sound held no humor. "I'm not disfigured. Only blind."

"Mostly blind," Felipe countered. "And anyway, what better way to take back the control. I know you despise the paparazzi for what they did to you. For what they did to your family. Are you going to let them have control of the story? Publish photographs of the Beast of Olympios and whatever headlines they wish to accompany it?

No, come now, Adam. The man I knew in school would not allow such a thing."

"And the man you used to know had a soul. Not to mention a face."

"If not for yourself, do it for Ianthe."

Had his friend been standing in front of him, Adam would have hit him for bringing his wife's name into this. But, at the same time, he couldn't deny he had a point. A point he had come to for himself already, but Felipe didn't know that.

"Take your control back," Felipe said. "Make this unveiling of your own making. Make Olympios yours again."

This was it, he realized. His moment. The power play.

The precise way and place to use his beautiful captive.

"When is this party?"

"In just over a month," Felipe said. "We can only hope my father holds on until then."

Adam could tell that Felipe didn't particularly hope any such thing. He knew that the two men had a complicated relationship, though he didn't

know the details. The three of them talked details as little as possible.

"I'll be there," Rafe said. "I have no reason not
to go."

"And you'll bring a date?"

"Absolutely not."

"I will," Adam said, his voice soft.

"You?" Felipe asked, not bothering to disguise
the surprise in his voice at all.

"Yes. I have a recent acquisition that I look very
much forward to showing off."

"Adam," Felipe said, "what have you done?"

"Just the kind of thing that suits a beast."

Belle was surprised when she was shown not to a
dungeon but to an elegantly appointed bedroom
with a four-poster bed covered by brocade curtains and festooned with pillows.

"I thought I was a prisoner?" She turned to ask
the servant.

She'd been made to surrender her phone, but
otherwise, everyone was being…nice to her.
Well, everyone except the Prince himself. She
doubted nice was a thing he did.

"There are enough rooms in the palace to keep even a prisoner comfortable," the man said drily.

"You don't approve of him," she said. "Do you?"

He lifted a shoulder. "He does not require my approval. Neither does he take any heed of my disapproval."

"Is he...is he crazy?" The disfigured man who had sought such destructive revenge on her father, and who had accepted her in trade could hardly be sane. Still, she felt like she needed to figure out exactly what she was dealing with.

He seemed to have a plan. A way he wanted to...use her to come back into the spotlight. She could only hope that plan meant there was a finite end to her sentence.

"He is not unaffected by the accident that caused those scars," the man said carefully. "That is about all I can tell you."

"Okay," she said, wrapping her arms around herself, shivering, because suddenly she felt cold. She turned to face the window, the small, narrow notch giving her a slight view of city lights reflecting on the sea. "Has my father gone already?" She turned again, to find her companion gone.

For some reason, the withdrawal of the servant made her feel isolated. Utterly alone. A chill swept over her, bone deep and intense. She had agreed to stay here, with a potential madman, for an unknown amount of time. There was no one here to protect her. Her father was likely long gone, and really, there was nothing he could do for her. He had to go and seek out his treatment; he couldn't stay behind.

She wondered if the Prince had even told him that she had traded places with him.

That thought made her stomach tighten. The thought that it was entirely possible no one would know she was here. She hadn't told Tony where she was going, because she'd known he would try to stop her.

No, no one would have any idea she was locked up in a medieval castle. What if nobody ever looked for her?

No. She wouldn't think of it like that. The way he had talked…he'd made it sound like he very much intended to be seen in public with her.

Which meant her being here wouldn't be a secret. But…

What would her father think? What would he do?

What would Tony do if he knew she was being held at some strange man's castle? She tried to imagine Tony taking on Adam. Her boyfriend's more…refined frame would be no match for Adam's monstrous form.

Adam was…

She thought back to that moment when he'd stepped into the light. That hard, scarred face. His incredibly muscular body. She shivered.

Thinking of him made her heart pound, made her skin tingle. It was a strange sort of fear. One that coursed through her veins like fire.

One that felt almost not like fear at all.

She heard heavy footfalls, and realized she had left the door open, had left herself exposed. She moved quickly toward the entrance, intent on closing it tightly, on giving herself some security. But, she didn't move quick enough.

There he was.

He was…she wasn't sure she had ever seen

a man so large. Six foot six, at least, broad and muscular. His face was even more shocking in the bright light of her bedchamber.

His dark eyes were watchful, and yet again, a window into how beautiful he might have been before he had been altered like this.

"Do I frighten you?" he asked.

"Isn't that your intention?"

"Not specifically."

He didn't elaborate, though. Didn't give her any idea of what he might be doing specifically. "So, do I go before a judge and jury? Or are you basically it?"

"This is my land. And I am the law of it."

"In other words, you can do whatever you want."

He nodded slowly. "Yes. In other words."

She drew herself up to her full height, ignoring the shiver that wound through her. "What exactly do you intend to do with me?" It took a lot of courage to ask that question, especially considering she didn't know if she wanted the answer.

"I intend to make you pay," he said, the promise

on those dark words licking down her spine. "But first, I should like you to join me for dinner."

"No," she said, the denial moving quickly from her lips, before she had a chance to think better of it. "I don't want to have dinner with you."

"Why not?"

"Because you're my jailer. Because I find you uncivilized."

"And hideous," he said, flashing her a slight smile, a brief glimpse of straight, white teeth, "I imagine."

There was no good way to answer that. He was...*hideous* wasn't the right word. Damaged. Terrifying. Compelling. But certainly not hideous.

"Show me anybody who wants to have dinner with the person keeping them captive," she said, rather than responding to his previous statement.

"That's the thing about being a captive," he said, his tone dry. "Choice is typically quite limited."

"What are you going to do if I refuse to go with you?" She planted her hands on her hips and took a step forward. She had to do this. She had to test him. Maybe he was a madman. Maybe he was going to go full Henry VIII on her. Off with her head, and all of that. Maybe he would do something even worse. But, until she tested the boundary, she wouldn't know what manner of man she was dealing with.

"I will pick you up, put you over my shoulder and carry you down to dinner whether you want to go or not."

"I don't want to."

Without missing a beat, he closed the distance between them, curved his arms around her waist and pulled her up off the ground, laying her over his shoulder. She was stunned. By his strength. By the ease at which he held her. By the heat of his body.

He was just…so very hot. And it burned her all over, even in places where they didn't touch. He moved, and she wobbled, grabbing hold of his shoulder to keep from falling. Then he turned and carried her from the room.

CHAPTER THREE

SHE WAS LIKE fire in his arms. That was all he could think as he strode out of her chamber, her lithe body wiggling over his shoulder as he carried her down the hall.

He braced one hand on her lower back, gripping her calf with the other. It had been three years since he'd had his hands on a woman. And suddenly, he was conscious of every one of those years. He had been far too lost in the bleakness of it all to think of it in those terms until this moment.

He had not thought of being with a woman. Hadn't thought of touching one. He had only been conscious of his bed being empty as far as it being empty of his wife. Not being empty in a way that meant it might need to be filled by someone else.

But now she was hot beneath his fingertips,

smooth, and very much alive. So different from the last time he had touched a woman and found her cold, icy and lifeless.

He gritted his teeth, clipping his jaw down tight as he continued to cart his protesting captive down the stairs and toward the dining room.

"How dare you?" she shrieked, pounding one fist against his back.

"How dare I feed you?" He laughed. "I truly am a monster."

"You could have sent me a crust of bread up to my room," she continued to protest.

"Yes, but alternatively you can sit and eat with me, and you can have lamb."

"Maybe I don't want to eat a baby animal!"

"Are you a vegetarian?"

"No," she said, sounding small, and slightly defeated in her response. "But still."

"If you have serious issues eating small, fuzzy things, you can always indulge in the vegetables and the couscous. Plus, there will be cake."

"I could have eaten that in my room," she said, wiggling, that movement of her body against his sending a jolt of sensation through him. He ignored it.

"No, *agape*, you could not have, because it is not on offer."

He stepped into the dining room, and set her down neatly in the chair next to his own. She looked up at him, her eyes wide. She truly was beautiful. Her dark hair was captured in a low ponytail, her blue eyes glittering in the dim light, distrustful, but nonetheless lovely. She had full lips, the kind he could vaguely remember enjoying back in the days when he had indulged in such pleasures.

Then, there was her body, which was pleasingly round in all the right places, as he had observed while carrying her from her room.

"What do you want from me?"

"I would like for you to eat. With the dramatics kept to a minimum."

She frowned, her expression stormy. "You did not allow me to trade places with my father so that you could feed me."

"No," he said, "perhaps not. I allowed you to trade with your father because you asked me to allow it. And as I mentioned before, I thought, that just maybe you might be of more use to me than a dying man."

She recoiled. So completely that it was nearly comical. "What sort of use?"

There was a time when a woman would have leaned in at such a suggestion, touched his hand, touched his arm, perhaps made things even more intimate by placing her hand on his thigh. But, those days had long since passed.

He let his eyes wander back to those beautiful rosy lips. And just for a moment, he imagined crushing his ruined mouth right up against them. Yes, she would most certainly take offense at that.

"Oh, anything I can think of. Propping up a wobbly desk, perhaps?"

Her eyes narrowed. "Be serious for a moment."

"Don't be silly. I'm always serious." At least, he had been for the past few years. Until these past few moments.

But, other than his friends, who he communicated with primarily over the phone, he only ever talked to his stripped-down staff. To Fos, the man who had been his father's right hand for as long as Adam could remember. And to Athena, his cook. Otherwise, the staff tended to rotate, and they kept out of his way.

Belle was one of the first new people he had spent any time with in longer than he could remember.

"Seriously deranged." She sniffed.

A few moments later, Athena appeared, along with kitchen staff carrying trays. "Tonight," she said, casting a swift glance over to Belle, "we have lamb with mint and yogurt, couscous and assorted vegetables. For dessert there is baklava."

"Thank you," he said.

Athena lingered.

Adam sighed heavily. "Have you something to say, Athena?"

"I don't approve," she said, her tone stiff.

"And I don't care," he returned. "Leave us."

Athena cast him a sad glance, and then turned the same look onto Belle. Then she shook her head and walked out of the room.

"Neither of your servants approve of you," Belle said, looking the food over critically.

"And my captive doesn't seem to fear me," he said. "I must be doing something wrong."

"I came all the way from California to face you down and get my father out of your dungeon. If I was going to freak out, I would have done it already." She tilted her chin upward, her expression mutinous. And a little bit too committed to defiance.

"We shall see. Eat."

He took his own command, digging into the food with relish. He picked up one of the lamb shanks, gnawing it close to the bone. He became aware a moment later of Belle's watchful gaze on him.

"What?" he asked.

"I assumed that… I assumed that royalty would have some sort of exemplary table manners. But, unless your customs are different here…"

He set the meat down onto his plate. "Are you determined to insult me at every turn? I served you dinner. I installed you in a very nice room. All things considered, I find you ungrateful."

"I'm sorry—am I not expressing adequate gratitude for my imprisonment?"

"You are a prisoner of your own design. You could have left your father here."

"Right. I could have left my father here to die."

He lifted a shoulder. "Plenty of people would have. A great many people possess more self-interest than that."

"My father raised me," she said, conviction in her tone. "He's all I have. And it might be easy for you to dismiss him as nothing more than a paparazzo, but he's everything to me. And you didn't even let me say goodbye to him."

"I'm hardly going to keep you captive for the rest of your life," he said. "Don't be dramatic."

"He's sick," she insisted. "He might die while I'm away."

Adam felt an uncomfortable stab of conscience. He was not in the market for his conscience to make any kind of resurgence. Not now. "I truly hope that isn't the case. However, he was well enough to sneak into my palace and collect photographs of me only a few weeks ago. Then he sold those photos and would do nothing to reclaim them. Tell me," he said, "since you are so well versed in matters of popular culture, do you know exactly how I got my scars?"

She looked down, shaking her head.

"All it took was a relentless photographer harassing my driver on a night with poor driving conditions," he said, his tone hard. "And in the end, damage was done that could not be undone."

He didn't see the point in bringing up Ianthe. If she didn't know, he wasn't going to discuss it. Not something so intensely personal. Not pain that belonged to him, and him alone, so unquestionably.

"I…" She looked away from him, and she had the decency to look ashamed. "I didn't know. I didn't. But, my father didn't endanger you."

"No," he said, his tone dripping with condescension. "He only broke into my home and invaded my privacy."

"He's harmless," she said. "I mean, I know that a lot of people don't understand the paparazzi thing. And I guess it can be a little bit…intense."

"They are nothing but leeches. Bottom-feeders who leech off the fame of those who have either talent or power."

"Fine. But my father isn't a leech. When my mother decided she didn't want me he took care of me. He's always taken care of me. And yes, he did it by taking pictures of celebrities. That's what fed me, all of my life. But nobody else was going to feed me," she said, her voice vibrating with conviction.

"There are plenty of other lines of work to be in."

"Says the Prince who was born with his job. Other people have to work. And not only that, they have to work hard to get work in the first place."

"Are you lecturing me on how hard life can be?" He sat back in his chair. "Excuse me while I get a pen and paper so that I can take notes."

"I'm sorry about your accident. My father didn't do that to you."

"But he was intending to use my personal tragedy for his gain." He laughed. "In fact, he has succeeded."

"Yes," she said, sputtering. "But it isn't that simple. He isn't doing it to hurt you. He needs help. He needed to be able to afford his treatments."

"Your justifications are hardly going to impress me. There is absolutely nothing I hate more than the press. Particularly the kind of fake press your father is a part of. But, it is of no matter to me. There is nothing I can do to prevent the publication of those photographs. Believe me—I have tried. But, I have figured out a way to take control of the situation."

"What's that?" she asked, clearly skeptical.

"I have not appeared in public since my accident. That's why those photographs are so valuable, you know. Because everybody's curious. How badly am I disfigured?"

She blinked. "You haven't been in public…at all."

"No. I think I mentioned when we first met—"

"When you took me captive."

"If you prefer. I think I mentioned that I have someone ruling in my stead. However, the time frame on our agreement is running out, and if I do not regain control of the country, a general election will result. And so it will be the end of the monarchy as we know it." He looked at the little woman sitting across from him and twisting her hands in her lap. "I would have thought you would have done a bit of cursory research on me before you tore off to my kingdom and offered to become my prisoner."

"There wasn't time. Whatever you think about my father, I hope that you can understand that I love him."

"Love doesn't matter except to the people it is between," he said, thinking of his wife. The press certainly hadn't cared that he'd loved her. They were always tormenting her, always working to dig up a scandal. "It is precious to no one else," he finished, the words bitter.

"Tell me. Tell me your plans. Since I clearly factor into them."

"I intend to keep you here with me, and then I intend to present you to the world as my mistress."

Belle felt as though she had been slapped. "Your... what?"

"My mistress. As I said, I have not been seen in the public eye since the accident. But, now those photographs are going to be published, and it is forcing me out of my seclusion. I suppose it had to happen eventually. I dislike greatly having my hand forced, but the timing coincides with an event that is politically expedient for me to attend."

He began to eat again, just as he had done earlier. There was something feral in the way that he handled his food. In his posture. He wasn't at all the way she imagined a prince might be. Though, when he talked about how long he had been away from the public eye, it all made a bit more sense. He had been here, she assumed. Nearly alone in this castle, answering to no one but himself. Clearly, performing for no one at all.

His manner was rough, his manners nonexistent.

Of course, she could expect little else from someone who had taken her prisoner over some photographs. Well, as a trade for a prisoner who was imprisoned for photographs.

And he had said he needed her for her beauty. So she supposed she shouldn't be shocked that this was where it was leading.

But a mistress. Such an old-fashioned word,

and certainly not one that had ever been applied to her.

She wasn't sure anyone would believe it. She didn't know how to act the part of a vixen. Or even someone mildly flirtatious.

She'd met Tony at school, and if not for him coming into the university library every day around the time she was studying, asking her what she was reading, the two of them would never have started dating. She'd been oblivious, and only his persistence had brought about the first date.

Oh. Tony. He would be…

"I can't do that."

"You don't have a choice. You agreed to be my prisoner, and so, here you are."

"But…but… I can't have the whole world thinking I'm with you!"

He lifted his hand, drawing his fingertips across her cheekbone, leaving a trail of strange fire in his wake. "Yes," he said, his tone dry. "I can see how that would be a grave humiliation for you."

He'd misunderstood, but she saw no point in correcting him. The why didn't matter. Not to him.

She looked down. "I don't suppose you would have a hard time finding somebody else who wanted to go with you."

"Yes," he said, "I'm very wealthy, and very powerful. But, a great many men are. And very few of them have my ill humor or destroyed features."

"So," she said, "you just want me to be your date?" Spoken plainly like that, it scared her slightly less.

"Oh, it is a bit more than that. I shall present you to the world as my lover, and with that there will be certain expectations. You will be required to keep up the farce or… I will continue to pursue action against your father."

She felt helpless. And she felt…well she felt like a prisoner. "I have a boyfriend." As if bringing Tony into the mix would discourage him.

"Not anymore."

Her heart twisted. "You can't just do that. I mean, you can't force me to break up with him."

"You don't need to do anything half so dramatic as that. But you will not be allowed to speak with him. In fact, I think I like this scenario even better. I hope he comes forward and complains to the media about the woman who jilted him for this." He gestured to himself.

"Why do you want this?" she asked. "Just to hurt me? Because of my father?"

"No," he said, hard and firm. "I need to return to the spotlight as I left." He laughed then, dark and merciless. "Which is difficult enough. And I will be damned if I allowed myself to be an object of pity. Of scorn. When I walk into that ballroom, in front of the world, it will be as though I never left. Yes, I am scarred now, but I will have a woman on my arm, and there will be no doubt that as easily as I stepped into your bed, I will step back into the throne room."

"And when...and when the party is over?"

He lifted a shoulder. "You will be free, of course. And we will concoct a story about our drifting apart. I could hardly settle down so quickly, after all. Someday, yes. But after a suitable succession of women such as yourself."

The arrogance, the confidence inherent in that statement should have enraged her. Instead she felt…hot.

"I need my phone back," she insisted, thinking again of Tony. Forcing her thoughts back to him.

"No."

"But, I have agreed to your terms."

"And yet, you are not a guest. You are my captive. I cannot have you making contact with the outside world that I don't approve of. You are the daughter of the lowest form of life that I can think of on this planet, and I have no guarantee that you are not also a photographer, or that you wouldn't also act as one if the opportunity presented itself. In fact, it would be rather a clever ploy, don't you think?"

She supposed it would be, but she honestly hadn't thought of it. "Well, I'm not. I'm getting my master's in literature."

"What do you do with a degree like that?"

"Teach mainly. But, my point is I don't move in that world. I don't condemn my father, but I'm not following in his footsteps either."

He spread his arms wide. "And yet, here you are. You followed in his footsteps close enough."

"I'm not hungry," she said, looking at her barely touched food.

"I still am."

"I want to go to my room."

He waved a hand. "You will go when I'm finished. I suggest you eat, because there will be nothing served to you after."

"I'm done."

"It is not in my best interest to have you show up at our big debut looking half-starved. I should like your curves to be able to fill out a ball gown."

Heat flooded her cheeks. "I don't care what you want my curves to do. They aren't yours. I'll put on a show for you, but you don't get access to my body."

The air between them suddenly seemed to freeze; then it heated again. He stood from his chair, moving over to where she was sitting. He leaned in and he reached out slowly, drawing his fingertip across her cheek. She was mesmerized, held captive by his face. By every groove and imperfection in his skin, by the twist at the corner of his mouth and that slash that ran over his right eye. With him this close, she could see that it didn't impact his vision. No, he saw. She had a feeling he saw so deeply into her that he could see just how fast her blood was rushing. How hard her heart was pounding.

"I will have access to whatever I like," he said, his tone soft. "And you would do well to remember that."

"I already told you—"

"You have a boyfriend. Yes. But, I have taken you prisoner in my castle, Belle. Ask yourself, do I seem like the sort of man who is concerned about whether or not someone has a boyfriend?"

"Given that..." She swallowed hard, trying to fight the fluttering in her stomach. "Given the fact that you have taken two people prisoner in the space of forty-eight hours, I imagine you don't care about things like boyfriends, no."

"You are correct." He settled back into his chair, and a wave of relief washed over her. But, she also felt a lingering chill from his withdrawal. "You see, it is an interesting thing, having everything taken from you. When you shrink your world down to a palace, to the grounds, it gives you a lot of time to reflect."

"Yes," she said, "clearly, you had your own *Eat, Pray, Love* moment and emerged extremely enlightened."

"Not entirely. Instead, I had a lot of time to think about what matters. And what doesn't."

"What matters to a man like you?"

"Survival. That's all that matters. That's the beginning and end of it. There are no rewards given for the manner in which you live, Belle. It would do you well to remember that."

"You have the audacity to comment on what my father does for a living while you say morality doesn't matter?"

"Because it hindered my survival. And, as previously stated, that is the only thing that matters to me. When you have nothing else, the elemental need to breathe is all that keeps you going. Yes, survival is the beginning and end of everything. When everything else falls away, the only thing that remains is that indrawn breath, and the seconds that stretch between it and the next. Sometimes, it is simply all you have to live for."

He took another bite of his dinner. "The living. Not the manner in which you live, not anything you possess. We are all creatures driven by that need."

She shook her head. "Not me. I like books. And I like the ocean. The sun on the sand, and how warm it feels against my skin." She saw something flicker in his dark eyes, and for some reason she felt her cheeks heat. "Those things are deeper than survival. And they matter. Because they're what make survival matter."

He laughed, but the sound carried no humor. "You would be surprised. There was a point in my existence when I looked around, and there was nothing. Nothing but an empty palace, dark, void of life. When every part of my body hurt, when I could barely get out of bed. And I would ask myself why I was still breathing. The answer was not books or the sun on the sand."

"What was the answer, then?" she asked, in spite of herself.

"Because I'm simply too stubborn to allow death to win. Sometimes, that's all the reason you have. So it is the reason that suffices." He stood then. "I am finished. Come. I will show you back to your room."

"I don't need you to."

"Yes," he said, his voice uncompromising, "you do. Because, I need to establish a few...ground rules."

She bristled. She wasn't accustomed to being told what to do. That simply wasn't the way her father had raised her. No, her father had seemed perpetually out of his element with a small child. But, he had loved her, and Belle had given him as little trouble as possible because she could see how hard he tried. Because from what she could remember of her life with her mother, she was much better off with her father.

He kept her on a very long leash. He had never imposed much in the way of strictures. She fixed her own dinner, chose her own clothes, decided when she would go out at night and when she would stay in.

Having this man suggest that she would be following anything like rules burrowed underneath her skin and prodded her.

Not that she'd ever done much with that freedom. But it was the principle.

Somehow, she managed to bite her lip and keep from saying something. But, the minute she did that fear crept back over her. A reminder that she didn't know who he was, not really. And didn't know what he was capable of.

It was so hard to take it all in; it kept hitting her in fits and starts, in little snatches. Probably because if it all landed on her at once, like a ton of extremely archaic bricks, she would lose her mind completely.

"If ever you are hungry, just let Athena know. She will feed you."

"I can't just…get my own food?"

"I never do," he said.

"Well," she said, "that is not particularly surprising."

She followed him down the long corridor, back to the stairs. "There is an exit that way," he said, gesturing to the left. "It will take you out to the gardens. You're welcome to explore anyplace you want on the grounds. Also, the ballroom, the libraries, all of that is open to you. But my quarters are not."

"Okay," she said, feeling a strange sense of relief. Really, she did not want to go to his quarters. Just the thought made her stomach clench up tight.

"My chambers encompass the east quadrant of the palace."

"An entire quadrant?"

He arched a brow, pausing midstride. "I take up a lot of space." Then he turned away from her and continued walking. That simple statement was truer than he probably realized. He most definitely took up a lot of space. And all the air in whatever room he was in.

"Can I at least...?" She took a breath. "You won't give me my phone. I need something. I need some way to get in touch with people."

"That is impossible. Not at the moment. I have my own agenda, and my concern is that you have your own, as well. I cannot have them conflicting."

He didn't sound the least bit regretful. "So you just intend to keep me cut off from the world?"

"It isn't so bad."

It was dawning on her, creeping up over her like a chill, that she was committed to staying here with a man who had not been outside palace walls in several years. A man who clearly didn't understand why anybody would have an issue being so isolated. It wasn't even an issue of him lacking sympathy or humanity.

He had no understanding. For why she might want more. For why she might need more.

A person could shrivel up into a husk and die here, and the master of the manor would never even have had the slightest inclination she was in danger of doing so.

"I don't…" It suddenly dawned on her when they approached her bedroom door that she had nothing with her. No clothes. "I don't have anything to wear." She had been wearing the same jeans and jacket since she had embarked on her journey yesterday.

"I can have something procured for you. You will get it tomorrow. Tonight, however, there is nothing I can do for you."

"But… I… I have nothing to sleep in."

He looked at her, his coal-black eyes burning through her skin, leaving her feeling hot, restless. "Then sleep in nothing. It is what I do."

For some reason, those words forced an image of him with acres of golden skin exposed. She wondered where his scars extended to. If all of him was so rough and tragically torn, or if parts of him were still whole.

And once more that strange sensation overwhelmed her. Made her scalp prickle, made her heart beat faster.

She gasped and jerked away from him.

He regarded her closely for a moment, and she sensed a strange current arcing between them; for some reason she was incredibly conscious and aware of the amount of restraint and strength it was taking for him to hold himself there, still and steady. She had no idea just what he was restraining himself from doing, or why she was so confident in her assessment of him.

She wasn't sure she wanted to know the answer to either thing.

"I will leave you," he said, his tone hard.

Then he turned away to go, and she found herself strangely wanting to stop him. To prolong the moment.

So she took another step away from him, holding her hands down at her sides and keeping herself resolutely still.

He walked away from the room, and back down the corridor. She let out a breath she hadn't known she'd been holding. And then she sprang into action. She forced the door shut, and locked it, hoping that it would hold. Then thinking it was probably silly because if anybody had the key to the door, it was her captor.

Her heart began to thunder hard, and she placed her hand against her breast, trying to catch her breath. She was shaking, shaking and trying not to cry. But then she wondered why she was bothering.

She let out a gasping sob, one tear trailing down her cheek. She turned and threw herself on the bed. She was alone. Really alone. Her father didn't know where she was, Tony didn't know where she was.

She had no way to reach them. She had no way to get help if she needed it. She simply had to trust the man holding her here.

Her wounded, strangely beautiful captor, who seemed to bring ice with him whenever he entered a room.

She closed her eyes, waiting for sleep to claim her. And as her thoughts began to swirl around in a confusing circle, she kept picturing his dark eyes. Dark eyes, set in a ravaged face, that were windows to an even more ravaged soul.

Thoughts of him made her restless. Made it impossible for her to breathe.

I will present you to the world as my mistress.

Memories of those words, of that voice, set off a quiver low in her belly. And her final thought before drifting to sleep was that if this was fear... if it was anger, it was unlike anything she had ever felt before in her life.

With those words still resonating inside her, she was forced to recognize, as sleep claimed her utterly, that she felt neither fear nor anger toward him.

But she refused to name the things she did feel. Which were far more monstrous than he could ever be.

CHAPTER FOUR

THE CASTLE FELT DIFFERENT. Adam had to wonder if it was because of the woman who was currently residing in it. He did not like to give her presence that much weight. There were often women and residents here in the castle, various staff members who he did his best not to interact with. Plus Athena, who had been with him for more than a decade.

Belle's presence should make no difference at all. And yet, it was as though he could feel her in the air. He gritted his teeth. Perhaps Felipe was right. Perhaps he was starting to get a little bit too close to insanity thanks to his years of isolation.

To be so much a part of a place that he could sense the presence of a new person…yes, that was perhaps a bit close to crazy.

Though, crazier perhaps, was that flash of heat

that had flared up when he had placed his hand on her last night. He should not have done so. It had touched something inside him, awakened something. Something that was far better left asleep.

For the first time in recent memory, he felt restless. Usually, he was content to conduct his business within the confines of the palace walls, or, if he was feeling like a change of scenery, on the grounds. Often, a burst of energy could be dealt with in his gym.

This was different. He didn't like it.

He prowled the halls of the palace, his staff members making themselves scarce the moment he approached. He was clearly radiating his foul mood.

If there was business to take care of as far as the country was concerned, Fos would have approached him already. But, he had not seen his adviser today at all, so that meant he lacked for specific direction.

Given the circumstances, he disliked that greatly.

A maid scuttled by, and Adam stopped her with

a warning look. "Have coffee sent to the library," he ordered.

"Forgive me, Your Highness, coffee is already there," she returned, bowing slightly.

"Why?"

"For…the lady. Was that not… Athena told me to serve her when she asked, and where she asked."

Of course she had. Obviously, his housekeeper had seen fit to override his handling of his own captive. "You did nothing wrong," he said. "You may go."

He continued on his way to the library. And there he found her. She was sitting in an armchair, her legs tucked beneath her, wearing the same clothes she'd had on yesterday. Yes, that was right; she'd told him she had nothing else to wear. He would have to ensure that something was procured for her.

Her attention was so focused on the book that was sitting in her lap that she didn't look up when he came in.

"Enjoying the story?"

She jumped, looking up, her blue eyes wide. "I

was," she said, her tone dripping with disdain. Her pale cheeks had a rosy flush to them, and he wondered if she was embarrassed about something. Or, if she was angry. Likely, it was anger.

"What is it?"

"Nothing you would be interested in," she said, closing it, keeping her finger tucked between the pages, holding her spot. She reached over to the table that was placed next to the armchair and picked up a mug that he assumed contained coffee.

Next to that mug was another, and beside that was an insulated carafe. He moved nearer, picked it up and helped himself to a cup.

"I was told I would find you here, along with the coffee," he said.

"And so you did." She gave him a sideways glance, her lips pressed against the edge of her mug, poised as though she was about to take another drink. "You said that I could go in any room I wanted, as long as I didn't invade your quarters."

"I did say that."

"Then why are you...prowling around looking vaguely disapproving? You're the one that wanted me here."

"Yes, *agape*, and you're the one who offered the trade. So a little bit less outrage from you would perhaps benefit us both. I gave you what you wanted."

"Well, preferable would have been to free both my father and myself."

He laughed and set his mug back down on the table. "But, that would benefit me in no way. You cannot expect me to do something simply because it is the right thing, can you?"

Adam had lost touch with what was right and what was wrong long ago. He would hardly allow this little waif to come in and lecture him when she had no idea what sort of man he was. No idea of the realities of the life he had lived. And the weight of his responsibility that was beginning to crush him now.

The simple truth was, he did have to get back out into the public eye. The more he pondered what Felipe had said, the more he realized his friend was delivering him the salvation that Adam had been looking for.

He had been mired in the darkness for too long.

But, for the sake of his country—because he certainly didn't give a damn for his own sake—he needed to change course. He had to take control, and he had known it was coming but…

Since the discovery that photographs of him had been taken it had been like he was walking out of a thick fog. The reality of the fact that the outside world still existed hitting him harder than it had in the past three years. The arrival of Belle and the phone call from Felipe had only cemented those things.

It had driven home what he'd known already: That it was time. That there was no question about whether or not he would take his rightful place.

"Well, I always hope that people will do the right thing," she said, her tone stiff.

"Come now, this facade doesn't suit either of us. Surely, you must assume that people will do what benefits them. Your father makes a living off that principle, does he not?"

She shifted, the color in her cheeks darkening. Yes, it was definitely anger. "I suppose."

"We talked about this already. Survival. That is why we're all here. To make it to the end. To prolong the distance between that moment of our birth and the moment we take our last breath, as best we possibly can. And if in between those moments we can find ways to thrive, then I suppose we will."

"I suppose," she said again, the words muttered darkly.

"But you must understand that it is not my own self-interest that pushes me here. But the interest of my country. Viceroy Kyriakos is a good man. But he is not a Katsaros. It is not his legacy."

"Obviously."

"It is time for me to make a stronger show for my country. For a while, I thought that a ruler such as myself would seem like a weakness to my people. That no one would want to see me so diminished. So, I was content to rule from behind the scenes. I did what I could to ensure that my people would not be a laughingstock, with a ruler who is disfigured as I am."

She winced at his words, but she didn't correct him. There was no dancing around the truth. He was disfigured. There had been a time when he and Ianthe had been media darlings in Europe, when they had been the most beautiful royal couple, the most photographed. But now he found himself without his princess, and without any appeal whatsoever.

It wasn't about vanity. It was about control. About the unknown. About giving this tragedy over to the world. He was reluctant to do so. For a great many reasons. But, his reluctance could carry on no more.

"And, as an added bonus, you will get to experience what it means to be on the other end of the photographer's lens."

She winced. "What do you mean?"

"Well, surely you have deduced that we will make the news—that was why you protested so last night, told me about your boyfriend."

"Well," she said, "yes."

"You have no idea the sort of headline we will create," he said. "Before the accident I mostly made waves here in Europe. But, the wider world will be interested in my return from the darkness, I have no doubt. As the deadline for my return approaches. Just as they will be morbidly interested in what horror the accident has brought upon me. I'm certain that there will be a salacious tabloid headline to that effect any day now. But, to emerge shortly thereafter, with a beauty such as yourself on my arm…well, that will be a story."

Again, he held off mentioning his wife. She didn't need to know.

"Of course, there can be no question about you making contact with your boyfriend. I can have nobody on the outside able to call the validity of this relationship into question."

"My father certainly won't believe it," she said. "And, even though he's likely in the hospital at this moment, he probably still has access to a phone."

"Really?" Tension gathered in his stomach, and he couldn't quite work out why. "You think your father won't believe that you came to speak to me, that I enticed you to stay. That I offered you beautiful clothing, jewelry…pleasure. That you were swayed by such things?"

She looked away. "Of course he won't believe that."

"Because I'm ugly? I assure you, Belle, a man in my position does not need to be beautiful. And a man with my skills doesn't need physical perfection to bring a woman to completion."

This time, when her cheeks turned red, he had a feeling it was from something else. The same thing affecting him. Molten heat that was coursing through his veins. For the second time in the space of twenty-four hours desire stirred inside him. What he was saying to her...he believed it to be true. Of course he could bring a woman pleasure in the dark. He didn't need his face restored in order to find all the places on her body that would make her cry out, that would make her wet with her need for him.

Again, the issue here wasn't vanity, but the desire to do so. It had been absent for long enough that he had thought it was another casualty of the accident. Another side effect of his loss.

Now he wondered. Now, with his body roaring back to life, he more than wondered.

In fact, he didn't wonder a damn thing. He was starving. That was what he was.

"I don't intend to find out," she said, her tone clipped.

"That's right. Because you have a boyfriend. How is he? *Pretty?*" She made a small, outraged squeak at that. "But does he know how to make you scream?"

She stood up quickly, holding her book up against her chest. "You're awful."

"I'm the monster who took you prisoner. If you expected me to be anything different, you were only going to be disappointed."

She gave him a look of pure umbrage, then made a movement like she was going to storm out of the room. He reached out, taking hold of her book, his fingertips brushing against hers, sending trails of lightning up his arm and down through the center of his body.

"You lost my place!" she shouted, her tone indignant.

"I'm sure you'll find it again." He turned the book over in his hands. "What is this?"

"Anna Karenina."

"Doesn't she get hit by a train?"

"Yes. At this moment it's something of a fantasy of mine. As it's preferable to my current situation."

He reached out, sifting his fingers through her hair. He expected her to pull away, to jump back. She surprised him by freezing instead. Her mouth dropped open, her eyes turning glassy. "I don't think that's true," he said.

"What? That I'm having a fantasy?"

"Oh, I believe that you're having a fantasy. I just don't think it has anything to do with being hit by a train."

He slid his hand to her cheek, drawing his thumb across her silken skin, brushing the edge of her lips. That seemed to mobilize her. She jolted, then pivoted to the side, stepping away from him. "I'm only here because I wanted to save my father. For that, I'll do anything. For right now, our only agreement is that I make an appearance with you at whatever event you feel I need a gown for. If you want something else, you're going to have to come out and say it. If you require my body, then I can lie down and take it, but you had better rest assured that it will be under sufferance. But don't play this game where you act as though you might be able to seduce me. That would be impossible."

"I've never had to force a woman into my bed yet," he said.

"I suppose that's hard for you to know, considering you're royalty and all. How can anyone refuse you?" She drew in a sharp breath and took a step away from him, and he thought for a moment that she was finished. But then she continued. "Also, I'm curious if you've propositioned a woman since…you know. You might find it more difficult now."

Her eyes glistened as she said the words, the color high in her cheeks, almost as though she felt guilty for landing such an unerring blow.

He was hardly going to let such an insult stand. He reached out, grabbing hold of her arm and dragging her back toward his body. She lost her balance, falling against his chest, her palms pressing against his muscles. She looked up at him, eyes wide.

He gripped her chin with his thumb and forefinger, holding her steady, and his mouth crashed down on hers.

CHAPTER FIVE

IT WAS A PUNISHMENT. There was no doubt about that. There was nothing ambiguous in the way his lips met hers, nothing gentle, nothing tentative. It had nothing to do with giving, nothing to do with pleasure. He tasted like rage. Maybe even hatred.

Belle was too stunned to do anything. Too shocked to fight back. So she stood, immobilized, trapped in his strong arms, pinned beneath the hard wall of his body.

He shifted, angling his head, forcing her lips open, his tongue sliding against hers. She gasped, and the action allowed him deeper access.

She waited. Waited for something like horror to overtake her. Waited for a surge of adrenaline, the kind that was supposed to come when you were in situations that were deadly. That gave you the strength to lift cars, and all other manner of things. Surely, some of that should come to her rescue now. Give her the strength to fend off one hard-bodied prince.

But it didn't. Instead, something else stole over her. A betraying heat, a kind of strange, languid feeling that started in her stomach and spread outward toward her limbs. It made her want to melt against him, and without being aware that she'd made the conscious thought to do so, she found herself doing just that. Curving her body around his, going pliant against the mountain that was Prince Adam Katsaros.

It was that strange feeling from before. That she had been calling fear. That prickling heat that spread over her skin. It came together here. In a brilliant flash. When his lips met hers, it became so very horribly clear.

His mouth might be too damaged to smile, but it had in no way affected his ability to kiss.

She had never imagined a kiss could feel like this. So raw, and rough and devastating. It wasn't good. It wasn't sweet; there was no connection in it. She had kissed only one other man, Tony, and the thing that she liked about kissing him was that it made her feel close to someone.

This was not that. This was hard, and it was angry, and it had breached her defenses and touched her in places she didn't know a simple meeting of mouths could reach.

And it made her heart beat so hard she thought it might tumble out of her chest. Made it impossible for her to think, impossible for her to breathe. Her knees went weak, and she curled her fingers around his shirt, keeping herself from melting into the ground as best she could.

He reached up, forking his fingers through her hair, curling his hand into a fist and growling as he tugged hard, changing the angle of their kiss yet again to something so impossibly deep it made her head swim. He growled again, and something in that sound pierced through the fog that had surrounded her.

What was she doing? Allowing this...this monster to kiss her like this? He had taken her father prisoner, and then he had taken her prisoner, as well. She had a man waiting for her back home who cared about her, who would be horrified to see her in this position and would never subject her to such a thing.

And here she was, betraying him, betraying herself. Allowing herself to be swept away on some crazy tide of physical need.

She pushed him, at his chest, his shoulders, but he was immovable. So she bit his lip.

He roared, pulling backward, his dark eyes fierce. "You will regret that," he said.

"My only regret is that I was in a position where it was possible to put my mouth on you in any capacity."

"And yet," he said, that ruined face of his contorting into a sneer, "you trembled in my arms."

She hated him even more for that, because it was true. Because she had felt…well, she didn't even know what it was. Some dark, sexual need she had not even been aware she possessed the capacity to experience.

"That's what prey does in front of a predator," she spat. "It trembles. Because it knows it's going to get eaten."

He laughed, and the dark sound reverberated in

her. Made her shiver. "Yes, indeed. A few more moments and I would have devoured you whole."

"You disgust me," she said, wishing very much that speaking the words would make them true. "No wonder you're alone! No wonder you've been hiding away from your country. Your face is the least of your problems. It's not the thing that makes you a beast."

She whirled around, running down the corridor as quickly as possible. She was blinded by anger. Blinded by fear. But the worst thing was, it wasn't him she was afraid of. She ran, not looking back, taking twists and turns in the labyrinthine set of halls that carried her to unfamiliar places she hadn't yet seen before.

Finally, she stopped, satisfied that he wasn't coming after her. She put her hand on her chest, trying to catch her breath. She looked around, stunned by the darkness around her. By the strange sense of abandonment here in this portion of the palace.

She took a cautious step forward, looking up at the paintings that lined the walk, seemingly laden with dust.

It was like she had wandered into a different building. No evidence of staff here at all, no evidence that anyone had set foot here in years. She moved over to a door and pressed it open slowly, looking inside and finding furniture that had been upended. A table lay on its side, a couch fallen over onto its face.

She closed the door again and continued on down the hall.

Then she saw another door, with a sliver of light coming from beneath it. Her breath caught in her throat, her limbs still shaking from the kiss, from the run, from...everything.

She looked back behind her, then back at the door. She tested the handle and found that it gave. She looked over her shoulder again, then quickly stepped inside.

The source of light was two wall sconces above the fireplace, casting a dim glow in the room. The curtains were drawn tightly shut, also covered in a slight film of dust that suggested they hadn't been opened in a long time.

There were bookshelves that were half-empty, a chair with a broken leg turned over onto its side.

One of the walls had a dark stain at the center, something that resembled an explosion of liquid, as though a glass had been thrown against it, the liquid spraying out.

She took another step forward, and saw a glittering trail of crushed glass that supported that theory. She wondered how long it had been there. Because, nothing about it looked recent, and yet, no one had cleaned it up.

She made her way farther into the room, her heart thundering so hard that she could feel the pulse echoing in her temples. She took another step, something crunching beneath her foot. She looked down and saw a vase, or, the remains of one. And there were roses, shriveled up and blackened, spread out among the broken shards.

She bent down, picking up one of the dried buds, brushing her fingertip over the shriveled and darkened edges.

She turned around, and saw a framed photograph facedown on the table the vase had likely fallen off. She reached out, touching the gilt edge gingerly, tilting it upward.

The image in the frame made her heart stop.

There was a woman, pale, blonde and beautiful with a wide smile on her face. There was a man standing behind her, looking equally joyous. His large hand was resting on her stomach.

Her rounded stomach.

She looked at the man, stunned by his beauty. By his sheer masculine perfection. But that wasn't what held her focus. It was his eyes. Those dark, piercing eyes that were all too familiar.

Adam. Before the accident.

She scanned the picture for clues. His left hand was on the woman's stomach, a wedding band on his finger. His wife. His wife, who had been carrying his child.

She knew two things for sure. There was no wife, and there was no child.

She gasped, pressing her hand up against her mouth, dropping the frame. It made a loud cracking sound as it hit the surface of the table, and she scrambled to reclaim it, to make sure she hadn't done any damage.

"What are you doing here?"

The low, steady voice, piercing the silence of

the room made her turn, the picture still clutched tightly in her hand.

Adam was standing in the doorway, his face dark with rage.

"I didn't...this is...these are your quarters, aren't they?" These quarters that looked uninhabited, that bore the evidence of fits of uncontrolled anger. This was where he lived. And it wasn't only her that wasn't allowed here. She had a feeling not a single member of his staff had set foot here since...since his accident.

"Yes," he said, his tone as dark as their surroundings. "I warned you not to come here."

"I didn't mean to," she said.

"Right, you simply found yourself in a part of the palace that was clearly separate and thought you would explore. Don't you think," he said, moving toward her, reminding her of a large predator, "that perhaps a place kept dark, with doors kept closed, should obviously be private?"

"I didn't mean—"

"The picture," he said, the words seemingly pulled from him, "give it to me. If you have damaged it in any way..."

She turned it so that it was facing her, and looked down yet again at the smiling faces. It wasn't the scars that made him look so different than he did in this photo. It was the bleakness. Something was missing from him now, extinguished. Gone completely.

"It's okay," she said, her hands shaking as she extended them, handing the picture to him. "It's fine."

"Set it down on the table where you found it," he said, not making a move toward it or her.

She complied, then moved away from it quickly, afraid somehow that by being near it she might do something to damage it. This thing that was clearly so precious to him. She felt awful, twisted up, shattered like the glass beneath her feet.

"I didn't… I didn't know," she said, her tone muted.

"And are you satisfied? Are you satisfied with seeing my loss? This," he said, drawing his hand across his cheek, "this is just a warning. A demonstration of what you will find if you look inside me. Honestly, it is a kindness. If I still looked like I did in that photograph, if I were unchanged…it would almost be worse. Better that I be destroyed both inside and out, yes?"

"You were married," she said, not quite sure why it came out that way. It sounded flat and stupid in the silence of the room once it was spoken.

"Yes," he returned. "You really should have looked me up before you came here. You might have learned some things."

"I know," she said, her breath freezing in her lungs. "But I… I just didn't…"

"That is why I don't allow paparazzi in my country. That is why I have no tolerance for it," he said, something in his voice fraying, unraveling as he spoke. "Do you think I would allow that scum to set foot in this place? After what they did to me?" His voice rose, along with his rage. "After they stole my wife from me?" He reached down, picking up a glass from the sideboard to his right. "After they stole my son?" He hurled the glass at the wall, and it shattered, leaving yet another pile of broken glass on the floor that she knew no one would do anything to clean.

She understood then. What she was seeing. It was the map of his grief. The evidence of moments when it had all become too much and he'd had to wreck his surroundings. Because his destroyed face wasn't enough. Because his destroyed soul wasn't enough.

"Adam…" It was the first time she had spoken his name out loud.

"Get out," he said. "Never come back here. This is not for you."

"I'm sorry…"

"Do you think I want your apology? Do you think I want your pity? Unless you can bring people back from the dead, you can save your breath. There is no resurrecting what is killed. There is no fixing this. There is no fixing any of it." He grabbed another glass, hurling it at the opposite wall. It exploded just like the first, the sound making her jump.

He took a step toward her, curling his fingers around her arm, holding her tight, so hard that it hurt. "Go," he said, "before I do something we both regret."

He released his hold on her, and she stumbled back, brushing her fingertips over her arm where he had just held her. She lingered for a moment, and she felt…she felt torn. He was scary, so of course part of her wanted to run.

But he was also injured, and not in the way that she had initially thought. It was so much worse. So much deeper. And a part of her felt broken in response.

Without thinking, she extended her arm, reaching toward him. He jerked back, like a wounded animal. "Go," he said again, his tone fractured.

And this time, she complied.

Adam considered taking dinner in his quarters. He rarely did that, because he did not allow anyone—even his housekeeper—to come into the section of the palace he had once shared with Ianthe.

But, then he realized that he was dangerously close to allowing Belle to dictate what he did in his own palace. The rest of the world had been closed off to him for long enough that he was hardly going to allow anything in his castle to be closed off to him, as well.

He figured she would probably avoid taking dinner with him anyway. So, when he walked into the dining room and saw her sitting in the same spot she had occupied last night, he was surprised.

After the kiss in the library, and the scene in what had been his wife's parlor, he had expected her to take refuge in her room. But, here she was.

"I hope there's cake tonight," she said by way of greeting.

"If you put in a request Athena will make sure there is cake," he returned, taking his seat next to her.

She looked down at her empty plate, and she kept her focus there until the dinner of chicken and vegetables was served. They ate in silence for a while, nothing other than the sound of silverware scraping over the plates sounding in the room. Then she sighed heavily.

"You wish to say something?" he asked, not bothering to ponder the fact that he could read her so easily.

"Yes," she said, "and I know that you probably don't want me to say anything, but I can't keep things to myself. It's hard for me."

"Really? Other people find it so easy. It's most

certainly not a matter of self-discipline and practicing restraint. By all means, do go and say whatever is on your mind."

"I'm not going to take a lecture from you about restraint, Adam," she said.

There was something about the way she said his name—about the fact that she said his name at all—that struck him like a blow to the stomach. How long had it been since someone had said his name to him when they were so near each other?

It was all so "sire," and "Your Highness," "Your Majesty" this and that. No one called him Adam except for his friends, and then it was only over the phone.

"I have a title," he said, as a reminder to himself most of all.

"Yes, I know. I could use it if you want."

"No," he said, deciding then that he would rather hear her say his name. "You are to play the part of my lover, and so you should seem somewhat familiar with me."

"Anyway. Adam. I am sorry. It makes more sense now. Why you put my father in prison for what he did. Why you don't allow paparazzi on the island. Why you don't have any patience or tolerance for it. You...you lost your wife in the accident."

"I didn't lose her," he said, his throat feeling scraped raw. "She died. Losing someone implies that you can find them again. Ianthe isn't missing. I'm not going to lift up a couch cushion one day and find her there."

Belle shook her head, a tear sliding down her cheek. She reached up and wiped it away, and he marveled at it. At the fact that this woman shed a tear for his pain.

"I do know that," she said, biting her lip and nodding. "It's a terrible thing to say. That your wife is dead. I can't imagine what it must be like to actually feel the loss. And she was..."

"She was eight months pregnant," he finished for her. "And, yes, our son died too."

She looked down, delicate fingers clenching into fists. "I wish you would have told me."

"Why?" He leaned back in his chair. "Because it makes me less of a monster? It makes you less my prisoner? Neither of those things is true."

"It makes me understand you. At least, a little bit."

"Do tell me all the things you understand," he said, keeping his tone deliberately dry.

For some reason, his stomach tightened. Thinking about her trying to understand. Thinking that she might just.

"The man that I saw in that picture…he wasn't a monster."

"No," Adam said. "He was one of the most celebrated royals in all of Europe. Renowned for his looks as much as for his temperament. He is a stranger to me."

He could barely remember being that man, and more to the point, he often didn't like remembering it. But, there were nights when he wandered down the halls, wandered down his memories, and ended up drunk in that room. It never ended well. It always ended with things broken. Just like his life.

"He's part of you," she said, her tone muted.

Adam shook his head. "He's not. He's dead, along with everyone else."

"Well," she said, softly. "I think that's terribly

sad. Seeing as you're still breathing and every-thing." She looked up at him, the steel in her blue eyes belying that softness in her voice.

"Have you ever lost anyone?"

"I might lose my father. I lost my mother emo-tionally when I was a child. That emotional loss? Well, that one hurts worse, in some ways. If my father dies, it isn't because he chose to leave me. My mother…she didn't want me. That's a par-ticular kind of pain."

"You don't know," he said, keeping his voice hard. "Until you have held someone in your arms while they die, someone you love, and felt them growing colder? You don't know."

He felt that cold spreading inside his chest now. That ice.

She cleared her throat. "I don't. You're right."

She reached across the expanse of table, placing delicate fingertips over the back of his hand. Her skin felt so hot against his. Especially in conflict with the memory of all that cold.

She began to draw away, and he pressed his other hand over the top of hers, holding her against him. For some reason, he was reluctant to break the contact. No, he knew why. He felt his body stir, heat flooding his veins where before there had been only ice.

She made him warm. She made him feel. And he wanted to cling to that. Wanted to cling to her.

Her eyes widened, and her tongue darted out and slicked over her lower lip, leaving it glistening, tempting. He could not forget the way it had felt to have her lips pressed against his. To delve deep inside her mouth and taste her, consume her.

There was something powerful in it. Something magical. Something he had not experienced in a long time. Touching another person, needing another person. At least physically. Yes, physically, he was ready for that.

He had spent a long time in this house, essentially alone, doing nothing to satisfy the growing hunger inside him. For touch. For a woman. Ignoring it so completely that he had been able to convince himself it no longer existed.

"I could try to understand," she said, the words broken. "I could try."

He lifted his hand from hers, reached out and

cupped her chin, holding her face steady as he continued to look at her. She was lovely, like a rose, beautiful as her name suggested. There was something simple to her, something wholesome. She was not overly made up, though that could perhaps be because of what had or had not been provided for her by his staff.

Her lips were red, her cheeks dusted with color. Like petals strewn across new-fallen snow. Something striking and rich against the stark white. He wanted to gather all that to himself, take it, taste it, make it his.

There was a time when he had been a man who had collected beautiful things. Who had *enjoyed* beautiful things. But he had forgotten that man, and he had forgotten that simple pleasure. He was remembering it now. But this need for her was different, it wasn't simply about collecting, but about possessing.

It struck him then that he didn't particularly want to take her out in public with him, drag them both into the light. Rather, he was much more interested in bringing her down into the darkness with him. Indulging in this yawning passion that had opened up inside him, seemingly endless, fathomless. So impenetrable that not even he could quite work out what it was, or what it would take to satisfy.

If he had just a few hours alone with her in the darkness, perhaps he could find it. Perhaps they could sate it. Together.

He leaned in, and she made a sound that might have been a protest, cut off by the firm press of his lips against hers. If it had been a protest, it wasn't evidenced in her response to the kiss. No, she didn't push back. Instead, she softened against him, a sigh escaping as she seemed to melt beneath his touch.

He didn't touch her anywhere but at that spot on her chin, where he held her firm as he continued the kiss, sliding his tongue along the seam of her lips until she capitulated, until she opened to him, begging him to take it deeper with that simple movement.

When he pulled away to catch his breath, she was trembling, the color in her cheeks even more vivid against the stark white of her skin. "I really do have a boyfriend," she said, her voice husky. "And I'm your prisoner."

"I can see how that would be a problem," he said slowly, "for you. I don't understand why I'm supposed to be perturbed by either."

"I suppose you wouldn't."

She did not sound outraged, however. She sounded drugged.

"I could make your stay here more enjoyable for the both of us."

She shook her head slowly, drawing back from him, removing her hand. "We should just eat dinner."

A lock of dark hair fell forward into her face, and she did nothing to sweep it away. He examined her, the gentle curve of her delicate neck, the stubborn set of her jaw, that subtle slope on her upturned nose. He watched her and said nothing all through dinner. She was his captive, it was true, but in some ways she was beginning to hold him captive, as well.

It wasn't good for a man to be celibate for so

long. In his grief, he had allowed himself to forget his physical needs. He would not do so again.

"What do you like?" he asked.

She blinked rapidly. "What?"

"You are not my prisoner," he said, not quite sure when he had decided to take this tactic. Perhaps when he had first felt her skin beneath his hands, how soft she was. Perhaps it had been then. "You will help me step out for the first time, and in order for us to accomplish all that we need to, all that I need to, I need for the two of us to be somewhat united. If we are to present ourselves as lovers to the world…it must be believable. The chemistry…*that*, I believe, will be the least of our problems. However, more than occasionally you look as though you want to finish the job my accident started."

She shifted uncomfortably. "I can't imagine that you would think I would have…easy feelings toward you. And just because I feel sorry for you—"

"You do not enjoy my kiss because you pity me," he said, his tone hard, firm. He had felt her melt beneath his touch, had felt her respond to him. That was more than pity.

At least, if he could be trusted to remember what desire felt like.

She went stiff. "There's no point talking about it."

"Because you're ashamed." He examined her more closely. "Is it because of my face?"

"No," she said, almost comically fast, "I'm not ashamed because of your face. I... I *should* be angry at you. And, I have a good boyfriend. He's very nice. I like him. You asked me what I like. I like Tony."

"I see," he said. "Your cheeks do not turn pink when you talk about him. They get pink when you look at me. When I kiss you."

"My face turns red when I get mad," she said, that stubborn jut to her chin even more pronounced than usual. "That's all."

"I could easily prove it's more than anger, Belle, though I imagine there is an element of that. If mostly anger at yourself. You want me." A lick of heat skated over his veins as he said it. As he allowed himself that confidence. There had been a time when he had been certain of a woman's desire for him. When he'd never had reason to doubt. He had never even put himself in that position one way or the other since the loss of Ianthe.

Doing so now…recognizing her need…it made him feel things he had thought long since dead.

"Impossible," she said, the word a hushed whisper. "Because I like Tony. And I like books. I don't like fearsome, angry men who seclude themselves in their palaces."

"No," he said, his tone sardonic. "You don't like me. You just pity me. Though, I have a feeling you would like to demonstrate that pity for me in a very physical manner."

She jerked back as though she had been slapped, and something in him regretted that. Regretted that step backward when he had been attempting to build an inroad. But she was making it difficult. Was making it impossible. She wanted him, and he didn't see why she was so intent on denying it. Certainly, she had a boyfriend, but he was back in California; he was not here. And, if Tony were a compelling lover at all, she wouldn't be so drawn to Adam.

When he had been with his wife it had been a simple thing for him to eschew the pleasures of other women. He had loved his wife and no one else, so no one else had tempted him. Belle, however, was tempted by him, no matter what she said about lovers and captivity.

"You really are kind of a beast," she said, standing up. He caught her wrist, stopped her from leaving.

"And what bothers you most about that? The fact that you would like to reform me, that you would like for your time here to mean something and you are beginning to see that it won't? Or is it the fact that you don't want to reform me at all, and that you rather like me this way? Or at least, your body likes me this way."

"Bodies make stupid decisions all the time. My father wanted my mother, and she was a terrible, unloving person who didn't even want her own daughter. So, forgive me if I find this argument rather uncompelling. It doesn't make you a good person, just because I enjoy kissing you. And it doesn't make this something worth exploring."

She broke free of him and began to walk away,

striding down the hall, back toward her room. He pushed away from the table, letting his chair fall to the floor, not caring enough to right it as he followed after Belle.

He caught up to her, pivoting so that he was in front of her. She took a step backward, then to the side, butting up against the wall. Then he caged her in between his arms, staring down at her. Her blue eyes were glittering, her breasts rising and falling rapidly with each breath.

"This is the only thing worth exploring. Not what could be, but what you have. The fire that burns between you and another person. For all you know, in the days since you've been here the entire world has fallen away. And if we were all that was left…would you not regret missing out on the chance to see how hot we could burn?"

She shook her head. "But the world hasn't fallen away," she said, her trembling lips pale now, a complete contrast to the rich color they had been only moments ago. "It's still there. And whatever happens in here will have consequences out there. I will help you, Adam, but I'm not going to give you my body. I'm not going to destroy that life that I have out there to play games with you in here. You're a stranger to me, and you're going to remain a stranger to me. I can pretend. I can give you whatever you need when it comes to making a statement for your country. But beyond that? I can't."

Then she turned and walked away, and this time, he let her go.

CHAPTER SIX

BELLE BARELY SLEPT. Her room was beautifully appointed, the bed plush and lovely, but after what had happened with Adam—again—she had been unable to relax. Not because she was afraid of him. If he wanted to force himself on her, he could have done it already. He would have done it already. It wasn't force that scared her.

It was the potential for seduction.

She shivered as she got out of bed. For the first time, she made her way over to the ornate wardrobe. When Fos had come in with her clothing yesterday she had simply asked for a comfortable outfit to wear, and then, last night when she had come back to the room after dinner she had dug blindly for a pair of pajamas.

She hadn't really examined the contents. She needed clothes, obviously, but she had a feeling the purchase of those clothes was all part and parcel to the mistress ruse.

All the better for rumors to abound about the sudden purchase of a woman's wardrobe by the Prince of Olympios's personal shopper.

The large piece of furniture was heaving with clothing. From lacy underthings to beautiful ball gowns. She could hardly believe it. Every item was more beautiful, more extravagant than the last. The fabrics were exquisite, so much so that she could scarcely bring herself to touch them. But then, once she did, she had a difficult time not touching them, because they felt so wonderful.

She and her father had lived a comfortable, simple existence in Southern California. Most of her life was spent in cutoff shorts and flip-flops, though, she took it up a notch by wearing jeans to class at school.

But mostly, she was accustomed to the more casual vibe of the West Coast of the United States. Certainly, she wasn't accustomed to things like this.

She dug around for a while until she found a

gray T-shirt that was made of material so soft it made the casual garment feel like a luxury. Then she found a pair of ankle-length black pants and a simple pair of black slip-on shoes.

She pulled her hair back into a ponytail and examined her reflection in the mirror. "Very Audrey Hepburn," she said to herself.

She wasn't sure why she cared what she looked like at all. In fact, she was mostly pretending she didn't care, which was why she had chosen the most unassuming pieces that had been provided for her. Because she didn't want to look like she was putting on a show for Adam. She didn't want to encourage herself to put on a show for Adam.

He was…well, he was barely civilized. He clearly didn't remember what it was like to be around people. Evidenced by his table manners. And his manners in general. He was tragic, his life story painful for her to even think about, even when she was angry with him.

No one should have to go through what he had gone through. To lose a wife and a child, an entire future in one night…it was more than any one person could be expected to bear. And, it was clear that Adam had not born it particularly well. He had been altered by it. Utterly and completely. So much so that he felt the man he had been was dead.

Her heart twisted, and she placed her hand to her breast, rubbing it slightly as she walked out the door of her bedroom. She didn't know what she was doing. Where she was going. To get food, she supposed. It was tempting in some ways to stay holed up in her room. To hide from him. But, then she really would feel like a prisoner. She needed to keep from going crazy.

And as difficult as it was to deal with him sometimes, she needed to continue to interact with him. So that she could play her part as lover to his satisfaction when they had to go to that party of his. So that he could begin to see her as a person and not simply a means to an end.

Or a means to his physical satisfaction.

That thought made her shiver. And she drew her arms tightly around herself as she continued to wander down toward the dining room.

She moved through the labyrinthine halls, and came around the corner, pausing in her tracks when she saw Adam standing there, large, imposing and more than a little bit terrifying. But not in the way he had been the first time she'd seen him. This was different. Deeper. Something that whispered in her ear that he was dangerous in a way she had never experienced before.

"There you are," he said, a dark light in his eye that made her feel…something. A kind of strange, shimmering heat that started in her midsection and radiated outward.

"Were you looking for me?"

"I was about to be."

She shifted her weight from one foot to the other. "I was just going to get coffee."

"It will have to wait."

"Come on now. Coffee waits for nothing."

"It will wait for me. I am Prince Adam Katsaros."

She couldn't help it. That made her smile. It even made her laugh a little bit. He frowned.

"Are you laughing at me?" he asked.

"A little bit. I suppose it's been a long time since somebody has laughed at you. So, it's probably good for you."

"That is open for debate. However, I have something to show you, so I'm not going to stand here and engage in one with you." He extended his arm. "Come with me."

She eyed him. "Suddenly you have manners?"

"Perhaps I'm beginning to remember them. As you remind me of other things long forgotten, as well."

"What is that?" she asked, stretching her arm out slowly and curling her fingers around his forearm gingerly.

"My desire."

She nearly drew back as though she had been burned, but he pressed his hand over hers and stopped her. His dark eyes burned into hers, and she really did feel like she was being scalded. From the inside out.

"I'm not sure what to say to that," she said.

"Well," he responded, "then I consider it a good topic of conversation. Because I think this is the first time I have successfully shocked you into silence. Did you suppose that I was entertaining women here in my isolation?"

"I know some girls like to think they're the

first, Adam, but I never really considered that I might be the first of your captives."

"You are. Until your father breached the security of my palace, no one has tried to draw me out of my seclusion. My story is far too tragic for such a thing. And, until your father, when the media realized they weren't going to get a story out of me, they left me alone. Actually, I imagine it's because the press caused my accident that they do leave me alone. It wasn't enough they had done it once before to royalty, but then they did it again. Things need to change."

"I know." She admitted that she had a little bit of a purposeful blind spot when it came to the kind of work her father did. Mostly because it had put food on the table all her life. And also because in her opinion her father was a good man. He did what he could in the economy they lived in. But…when things went this far, when they put people in danger, cost people their lives, he was right. It had to change.

"You know," she said, still clinging to his arm as he led her down a hall she hadn't been in before, "my father wasn't always a paparazzo. He used to travel around and take pictures of world events. Go behind enemy lines, all of that. But, then he ended up taking care of me, and he couldn't travel the way that he used to. Plus, it's hard to make a living that way. People don't like to see how ugly the world is—they would rather get a look at the beautiful people. And yes, to a degree get a look at the ugly side of the beautiful people so that all the normal ones don't feel like they're quite so bad off."

"Well, I will certainly have that effect on the masses. A little bit of tragedy porn to go with dinner."

"You make me see the other side of it," she said. "Not just the fact that sometimes the photographers go to dangerous lengths to get the picture, but…the fact you didn't do anything to have your privacy invaded like this. Apart from the accident, nobody has a right to you. They don't own you just because they know your name."

"Well, thank you for that stamp of approval," he said. "Without it I'm not sure how I would have held to my conviction that I was entitled to my privacy."

She stopped moving and stamped her foot. "I'm trying to tell you that you changed my mind. Maybe you could be a little bit nice about it."

"Maybe," he countered, "you could stop expecting me to be nice."

She huffed. "I should."

They stopped at a pair of double doors at the end of the hall, and she looked at him questioningly. "I have something to show you," he said simply. Then he pressed his palms flat against the doors, pushing them open.

The room was dark, curtains that stretched from floor to ceiling covering all the windows. He turned, pressing a button, and she heard the faint rustle of fabric, followed by a shaft of light piercing the darkness. All the curtains began to part, revealing bookcases. Everywhere. Extending from the high arched ceiling down to the marble floors, ladders stationed every few feet, to allow access to the upper shelves.

"What is this?"

"The library."

"But, you said that I was in the library yesterday." She turned in a circle, feeling awed by her surroundings.

"You were in one of the libraries. This is the main library, the one that houses my entire family history. The history of the country. Additionally, every great work of literature to come out of Olympios. Also, classics from the rest of the world. There are some modern works of fiction over here…popular works and more obscure works. If it's been written, it may very well be in here somewhere."

"I don't…why are you showing me this?"

She turned to look at him, at that scarred, rough face that was starting to become familiar to her. He was no longer shocking, and she didn't view the ridges on his skin as imperfections. Rather, they were simply a part of him. And those eyes, dark and fathomless, containing a wealth of pain…they made her feel.

"You said you liked books," he said, his voice flat.

"So I did," she said, taking a tentative step forward, walking to the nearest shelf. She let her fingertips drift over the spines, marveling at the collection in front of her. "Of course," she turned back to him, trying to steel herself against the feelings that were rioting through her, "I also said that I liked my boyfriend," she pointed out, "but, he didn't materialize. Neither did a way for me to contact him."

"Sadly," he said, "that is still not possible. However, I would like to point out that you look far more enraptured when you talk about books than you do when you talk about him. And, frankly, you look more excited when you kiss me than you do when you speak about this other man."

"It's not all about excitement," she said, her tone dry. She sounded prudish to even her own ears. *How annoying.* "Sometimes it's just about feeling taken care of. Feeling like someone is there for you. They're stable. He cares about me. I feel like we have a future together. When I'm done with school." She ignored the fact that she didn't feel the kind of churning sexual excitement that she felt when she was around Adam. Ignored the realization that hit her just then that suggested if she felt even half what she felt for Tony as she had felt for Adam over the past couple of days, there was no way she would still be a virgin. Resisting Adam—who had taken her captive, who was hard and scarred and nothing like anything she should be attracted to—was much harder than anything ever had been before. But somehow, she had managed to resist Tony for eight months of dating.

Adam wasn't wrong. She did find books more exciting than she found Tony. And that was somewhat problematic, she realized.

"Passion is a key part of love," Adam said. "And if not of love, then at least of life. My life… what you walked into, that is what life looks like without passion. It is dark, and it is isolating. You have not lost anyone the way that I have. You could have passion. Why don't you?"

"I didn't say we didn't have passion. I just said passion wasn't everything. My mother…she… she's famous. Well, she's the daughter of a very famous actress. And she essentially paid to have me swept under the rug. My father could make a spectacle of her, I suppose, but it would compromise certain things that were put in place for me. And, not only that, it would drag me out

into the press, and he doesn't want that for me."
She laughed. "I suppose that highlights the fact
that he does see what he does as an invasion of
privacy, since he wouldn't want it for his own
daughter. But my point is she's the kind of person who follows passions. Drinks deep of life,
and does all that stuff that's fun and New Age
sounding. But, she didn't do anything with her
responsibilities. She didn't want to take care of
her own child. I would rather have stability. I
would rather have security than anything so ca-
pricious as passion."

"I suppose you have felt loss," he said, something changing in his expression. "I underes-
timated that." He shook his head. "Emotional
passion... I have no desire to experience such a
thing again. Hope destroyed is something best
never resurrected. But physical passion..." He
took a step toward her, that light in his eye turning predatory. "Getting caught up in that, getting
burned by that...that is something that I miss.
And I wonder, have you ever experienced it?
What does your boyfriend make you feel, Belle?
Is he a pretty-boy surfer? Or maybe just a model

with soft hands. A hollow chest and that kind of hungry look about him with sunken-in cheekbones. That's very Californian, isn't it? Probably nice to look at, but does he know how to touch you?"

His voice grew rougher, lower as he drew closer. "I am not a pretty man—that point can't be argued. But I would know how to touch you. I can give you so much more than just a library. I can make you forget your name while you call out mine. Can he do that? Three years. Three years and I haven't wanted another woman. How could I? My wife…she was beautiful. And more than that, I loved her. But I am tired of having an empty bed. I'm tired of walking around with all this fire inside of me and nowhere to spend it. Something tells me you're more like me than you would care to admit."

Belle couldn't breathe. She was lost in this moment, lost in him, in the tendrils of flame that wrapped around her with each word he spoke, stoking the heat inside her hotter, higher.

It wasn't him she was afraid of. No, it really wasn't. It was herself. Because for the first time in her life she wanted to reach out and take the reckless thing. The wrong thing. She had always felt so grateful for the stable environment provided by her father. Because she could remember living in her mother's house. Living in all that turmoil until she had been shunted off, sent to live in that little beach bungalow with her dad.

And there at least had been stability. He had loved her, once he had known she existed. He had taken her in gladly. Then she had met Tony at school, and he had seemed perfect in that very same way. Nice. Caring. Patient.

Adam was none of those things, and yet she felt like she was perilously close to being carried away on a tide of something that felt a lot like lust.

"Tony is very nice," she said, the words sounding as bland as Adam had implied her boyfriend was.

"I imagine he's very nice in bed, as well," Adam said.

He did not say "very nice" as though it was a compliment.

"He...he respects me."

"That's very interesting. What does it mean, I wonder? Does it mean what I suspect? That he doesn't want you? At least, not in the same way that I do. Which has somehow been conflated with respect. An excuse, perhaps, that allows women to put up with tepid bedroom experiences?" He laughed. "Respect. Synonymous with beige walls and sex once a week that takes less time than the human-interest piece on the evening news."

Her cheeks got hot. "No," she said, "that isn't what it means."

"Oh, I think it does in some circles. Why is it that respect is never equated to a man worshipping his lover's body? To being so hungry for her he can be satisfied by nothing else? In my opinion, if a man you're sleeping with respects you, he should respect you enough to make your knees weak and your throat raw from screaming his name all night."

She didn't correct him and say that he was respecting her desire to wait to be intimate. She didn't know why she held that bit of information back. Possibly because her airway was currently constricted, and it was making it difficult for her to talk. And her thoughts were a little bit jumbled, which made forming sentences difficult, as well.

She didn't want to tell him that she had no idea what he was talking about. That she had never screamed any man's name in her entire life. And that she wasn't exactly sure what could feel quite so intense that it would induce her to do that.

It hit her then, that the low, twisting sensation in her stomach, the slow, long pull that she felt starting there and moving down lower, was connected to a deep desire for him to show her.

It was embarrassing, just how innocent she was. How little she knew. She blamed her mother in that regard. Not just her absence, though, it wasn't as though her father wanted to sit down and have a conversation with her about the facts of life.

No, she wasn't sheltered. That wasn't it. It was just that she had chosen, deliberately, to ignore as much about that sort of thing as she could. Because she connected her mother's abandonment with passion. A passion for life, for men, for money and clothes and parties that had been severely curbed by the addition of a young child to her life.

So, Belle had resented it. All of it. She had clung to her simple existence, to being happy with what she had. The breeze blowing in off the ocean, the feel of a book in her hands. Dating Tony was an experiment, for sure. She enjoyed his companionship, she liked kissing him, but she had shied away from the rest of it because she was afraid.

Afraid of something she hadn't quite been able to put a name to. But, she could put a feeling to it now. It was fire. That fire that Adam ignited low and deep inside of her. A fire she was afraid—once it was able to burn freely—would never be extinguished.

She was afraid she would forget herself. Forget who she was, and what she had once wanted. Because certainly, that was the fate of her mother. Who had forgotten about love, and about the important things, because of that restless fire.

She also realized that while she was rejecting all of it internally, while she was keeping silent to avoid drawing herself in deeper, she also wasn't running away. No, she was standing here in this library, in a shaft of light, with Adam advancing on her, his dark eyes glittering. Just standing there, doing nothing to try to put distance between them.

She wanted this. She wanted him to take control. To make it so the decision was no longer hers. She was too afraid to decide on that last step. To close the distance between them. To admit to herself that she wanted to know. That she wanted to know what might make her cry out his name, and that she wanted it to be his name specifically.

How was that fair? How was that possible? When Adam had taken her father prisoner, taken her captive, as well? When she had a nice, sweet, patient man waiting for her back in California? How could she feel any of these things for this dark and tortured soul in front of her?

She didn't know. Perhaps, it was that element of helplessness. Of the choice being taken from her. Perhaps, that was why it felt possible. Why it felt necessary.

In this castle, removed from the reality of the world, far removed from that little piece of the world she had carved out for herself. From school, from friends, from books and boyfriends. From the familiar California coastline and the easy breeze that blew through there.

She was in his domain. His country. This mountainous island nation, where the wind ripped sharply through the crags and peaks of the unbending mountains, where it whistled around the turrets of the palace and created a sense of restlessness rather than a sense of ease.

It was also far removed from reality, like something in a fairy tale.

Or, something from a fantasy that she would never have allowed herself to have anywhere else.

"I like it when you say my name," he said, his voice rough, the dark notes skimming along her skin, making her shiver. "I should like it even more if you said my name in bed."

She looked up at him, her lips feeling suddenly dry. She slipped her tongue out, traced the edge of her own mouth. And suddenly, she was very aware of the fact that he had done the same the last time he had kissed her.

She didn't think that she had been drawing his attention to her mouth intentionally, but when his gaze sharpened, when his focus moved lower, she wondered. Questioned herself a little bit more deeply than she wanted to.

Yes, she was trying to remove her own culpability in this situation. But, if she were honest… and then she couldn't think anymore.

He reached out, his fingertips brushing her chin, tilting her face upward. Then he traced along the line of her jaw, to her lower lip, following the path her tongue had just forged. Then he continued on, at the other side of her face, along her cheekbone and back again, to that delicate spot just beneath her ear, and down the side of her neck, which made her tremble.

Those strong hands on such a vulnerable part of her should have been terrifying, or at the very least somewhat repellent. But, she found herself entirely unrepelled. Instead, she wanted to melt into that firm touch, encourage him to take an even firmer hold on her.

She gloried in it. In his strength, his power, next to her delicate frame.

She couldn't explain it. She couldn't even rationalize it to herself. But, that didn't make her move away from him. Didn't entice her to break their contact.

She looked up, meeting his eyes. Those eyes that she had seen lit with happiness in a photograph, but were so dark now. She lifted her hand, her fingertips brushing the rough skin on his cheek. Then she drew back quickly, as though she had been burned.

Adam reached out, curving his fingers around her wrist, holding her tight. He raised her hand slowly again, placing it back where it had been a moment before. There was something needy there, written across his face.

She adjusted her position, so that she was facing him square, both of her hands on his face now, resting just above his jaw. Her thumbs touched the corners of his mouth, and a deep sound rumbled in his chest. Something that sat between a growl and a purr of satisfaction.

Her fingertips brushed up against the scar tissue next to his lips, but she didn't flinch. Didn't pull away. She hadn't known him before. Yes, she had seen that photograph, but it wasn't the Adam she knew. It wasn't the Adam she found so compelling. It was a piece of the puzzle that was the man who stood before her, a piece that mattered. That meant something. But, it certainly wasn't what compelled her. The idea that he had been a more beautiful man once.

He was the man who drew her in now. The man who compelled her to leave behind a lifetime of restraint. The man who made her question so many things about herself. About what she wanted.

He dropped his hands to his sides, then reached out, grabbing hold of her hips and holding her steady as she continued to touch his face, slowly, softly.

She raised her hand, sliding her thumb down that thick ridge that ran through his eyebrow, down along to the edge of his eye. "You can see all right?" she asked.

"Yes," he responded. "Lucky, I suppose. Though,

I have never considered much about the accident to be lucky."

"Well, I guess *lucky* might be a stretch. But not adding more trauma by losing your sight is certainly something."

"Honestly, I would not have cared. Until recently, there was nothing to look at." Those words sent a spiral of pleasure winding through her. She tried to remember if Tony had ever told her she was beautiful, or ever implied it the way that Adam just had. If he had, it didn't stand out to her. But, she knew for a fact that Tony had kissed her, and right now she couldn't remember it at all.

She could only remember what it was to kiss Adam, which was something else entirely. Something new. Something fully unto itself.

"In all of this darkness… I had forgotten that I could see," he said. "Looking at you—at your beauty—it reminds me. You remind me of the few pleasures that are left to be had in this world."

Sex. He meant sex. Nothing deeper, nothing more lasting than that. And even if he did, she couldn't leave her life, she couldn't leave her father, and…what? Marry the Prince of some small island country? A man she barely knew? *No.*

So it was fine, really. That he was only talking about the physical. Because it was the physical that held her in thrall at this moment, surely. It certainly wasn't anything else. Certainly wasn't anything deeper. It couldn't be. It was impossible.

She wasn't sure that it mattered. At least not now.

Because whatever this was, it was stronger than anything else. Stronger than any other force, than anything tethering her to the past, or reminding her of the future. This moment, this feeling, this need, was bigger, brighter, fiercer than anything could ever be.

"Adam…" And she didn't know what else to say. Because the feelings, the need, had grown too big and it blocked out all the words, all the things that were spinning around in her head. She wanted to tell him that he wasn't ugly. That he might be a beast, but that she wasn't certain she cared.

Words fled, but desire didn't. And so, keeping her hands on his face, she pulled upward onto her toes and leaned in, closing the distance between them and taking his lips with her own.

It took only a moment for Adam to claim control. For him to wrap those arms tightly around her and press her back against one of the bookshelves, a shelf digging into her lower back. She didn't care. She didn't care at all. Not about the discomfort, not about anything but the hot, hard press of his mouth against hers.

But this time, his hands did not stay contained to one place. This time, those large, warm hands roamed over her curves, sliding up to cup her breasts, his thumbs moving over her nipples. She gasped, arching against him, ignoring the slight pain when her shoulder blades met with the corner of a book.

No one had ever touched her like this. No man had ever touched her there.

She should be outraged, she should be…something. Virginal. Afraid. She didn't feel any of that. She felt completely caught up, swept up in this madness that had rolled in between them like a cyclone.

Then his hands moved lower, gripping hold of

her hips tightly, drawing her against the hardness of his body, showing her the evidence of just how much he wanted her. She moved her hands, sliding them around behind his head, then pulling herself closer until she was wrapped around him.

His hands moved lower still, down beneath the waistband of her pants, between her thighs. She gasped as his fingertips slid over the smooth, silken fabric of the panties she was wearing. She was…well, she was terrified of the feelings that were rioting through her, but she was also completely enraptured by them. He pressed harder, and she could feel dampness gathering there, and she wondered if he could feel it too, through that thin fabric as he continued to torture the sensitive bundle of nerves.

She forgot to be horrified. Forgot to be embarrassed. There was nothing but the fierce, blinding need that he was creating with the magic of his touch, with each pass, each stroke. She arched against him, moving her hips in time with the movement of his wrist.

She was shivering, shaking, a coil drawing tight down at the base of her spine and spreading down even farther, internal muscles she hadn't been aware of before pulsing as he continued the sensual assault, continued kissing her, long and deep, his tongue sliding against hers. Continued stroking her between her legs, amping up her arousal to an impossible capacity that she hadn't known existed inside her.

Then one fingertip drifted beneath the edge of the fabric of her panties, his hot skin making contact with her slick flesh as he drew his finger slowly forward, using her own wetness to ease the friction while he tormented the source of her desire.

And she broke. Shattered utterly, completely, waves of need washing over her, followed by shivers of satisfaction that went deep and seemed to ebb and flow on and on. She couldn't take any more; she was sure of it. But she didn't have the words to say that, couldn't form a coherent thought. And so, he didn't stop. He moved forward, pressing one finger deep inside her, the invasion so intimate, so unexpected that she cried out.

"Adam!" Then he rocked his palm forward,

pressing down hard on the place where she ached for him. She had been wrong before. She hadn't shattered. That had only been a crack. Now she shattered completely, reduced to nothing but glittering dust at his feet as she cried out his name over and over again, clinging to his shoulders as the intensity of her release swamped her, left her knees weak, left her body spent.

And when it was over, her throat was hoarse from calling out his name.

She understood why now.

She forced herself to meet his gaze, her cheeks turning pink as she did so, as she looked at the pure, unmitigated hunger in his dark eyes. Oh, yes, she understood. Why women lost their minds for passion, why they would spend their nights gladly with a man like him, and forget everything else.

And it was that that had her wiggling out of his embrace, fighting to get free, to get some distance.

"I need to..." She gasped, trying to take a breath. "I can't breathe."

He let go of her, taking a step back, his hands

raised slightly as though to demonstrate that he was going to allow her this distance.

Her eyes filled with tears, her whole body beginning to tremble. She felt...well, in spite of the fact that she was fully clothed she felt naked. Exposed. He hadn't even seen her body, but she felt as though he had seen something even more private, something that she had kept hidden, desperately, even from herself.

"I need coffee," she choked out.

And then she ran from the room, leaving behind the first man to make her understand passion. The first man to ever make her confront what she had always feared about herself.

That given the chance, she would prove no better than her mother, no better at all.

CHAPTER SEVEN

BELLE AVOIDED HIM rather skillfully over the next few weeks. And his body rebelled against it. But, Adam himself thought it was perhaps best not to push. He had to keep his eyes focused on the prize before him. Which was the party, and his great debut to the public.

His Viceroy had announced that Adam would be making a public showing, and had intimated that it was time for Adam to resume his rule.

All was going according to plan.

Other than those photographs, hastily published the previous week.

But, they had been poor quality, and while the story had certainly created a sensation, it hadn't done as much damage as he'd thought they might. They had also paled in comparison to the real story. The fact that he had decided to step back into power.

Ultimately, the real control was still with him. He had a chance to write the next headline, and it would all come down to how he—how they—presented him on the world stage.

Considering that, he needed to keep Belle from looking like she was terrified of him. As she had looked at him in the library. He had to wonder if she was afraid of him, or if she was disgusted with herself. For losing herself in the arms of a man who might as well be a beast. Who was wholly unattractive and possibly the absolute opposite of the man she fancied herself in love with.

He was not vain. But for the first time he allowed himself a moment to mourn the loss of his looks. Now that he actually wanted to seduce a woman, it mattered.

Of course, in many ways he had seduced her; it had just left him unsatisfied. Had he been thinking clearly, he would have ripped her clothes from her body and buried himself inside her before satisfying her the first time. That way, they might have both come to a better conclusion.

He scowled, pacing the length of his room. Felipe's party was tonight, and Adam was wearing a tuxedo for the first time in years. A new one had been made and fitted for him just this week. He'd had nothing to do over the past three years but spend time working out in his gym, and he was far too large now to fit into the suit he had once worn.

As Fos finished straightening his tie, Adam looked at his reflection and thought it fitting. That he could no longer even wear the clothes he had once worn, and that the more streamlined physique he had once sported was also gone.

Three years ago he'd had the sort of aristocratic form suited to a tuxedo. And the face to go along with it. Now, even with a suit that had been custom made, he looked like a panther being dressed up as a house cat. And his scars certainly didn't help.

In some ways though, he found it fitting. Why should he step back into this life with case? Looking as he had? He had changed. Utterly and completely.

"You might consider being a bit nicer to the girl," his adviser said, partly under his breath, as he brushed something off the shoulder of Adam's suit jacket.

"I gave her a library," Adam said.

"Yes," Fos returned. "And yet, she still avoids you as though you carry a particularly virulent strain of the plague."

"I'm a monster—haven't you heard?"

"It is not your face that makes you a monster, Your Highness."

"I don't think I asked for a commentary," Adam said.

"You didn't. But, you intend to make your debut with her tonight, and it might be best if she didn't look afraid of you."

"I have no control over that. I have done my best, at least, as well as I can do under the circumstances. The circumstances being that she is my prisoner."

Fos nodded. "I can see how that might make it difficult. Perhaps, make an effort to appear human. That might help both with Belle and with the ball."

"I didn't say I needed help with either."

"But you do."

Adam snorted. "Trust me. It isn't that she doesn't like me. It's that she likes me a little bit too much."

"Yes," Fos said, "I get that feeling. But how are you going to entice her if you don't remove the fear?"

"Some women like fear."

"Some women who are not as sweet as she is, I think."

"I don't want her to like me," Adam insisted. "I might want her in my bed, but that is a different matter."

"You're determined, then. To stay under this curse? To stay miserable? Because I think she's the one that could fix all of this."

Adam turned to his friend, forcing a grim smile. "There is no fixing this. What's done is done. All I'm after is a little bit of satisfaction, if it's on offer. And a chance to take back my reputation. A chance to assert myself as a strong leader for my country. I'm not asking for anything else."

"And if you could?"

"I have no interest." He looked back at his reflection, a reflection that he didn't often ponder. What point was there? All he could see on his face was a road map of the destruction that had been wrought in his life. He didn't like pondering it at all. "I suppose," he said, "this is as good as it gets."

"You have yet to see your date," Fos said. "Believe me. She is as good as it gets."

The old man had not been wrong, neither had he been exaggerating. When Belle appeared in a golden gown that conformed to curves he had had his hands on, glittering like a trophy, her dark hair swept to the side, cascading over her bare shoulder in ringlets, he felt as though he had been punched in the gut.

Arousal that had been with him, clinging to him, gnawing at him like a wild beast made itself known all the more as he looked at her. He wanted her. He wanted her more than he had wanted anything in the past three years. In truth, she was the first thing he had wanted in all these years. Because there had been nothing he wanted beyond drawing the next breath since his loss.

But she was a hunger. Fierce and unquenchable.

He extended his arm, and she looked at it as though he were offering her a snake. "Come," he said, his tone much harder than he had intended. "You can't look afraid of me when we walk into the ballroom. It will not do."

"I'm not afraid of you," she said, stepping toward him, the dress swishing around her legs. "There." She looped her arm through his. "See?"

He led her through the corridor, more brightly lit than usual. The double doors to the palace opened wide, and outside was a car. He had a strange sort of flashback, a return to a life that lived only in dreams now.

He stopped, a sudden lump in his throat surprising him, an ache that started there and extended all the way down through his chest, immobilizing him.

"What's wrong?" she asked, looking up at him with luminous blue eyes.

"I haven't… I haven't actually been in a car since my accident. Not that I can remember. Yes, I got a ride home from the hospital, but I was heavily sedated at the time. Otherwise, all my treatment has occurred here at the palace."

She tightened her hold on him. "Are you afraid?"

He shook his head. "No."

It was just that this felt a lot like the night he had left the palace with Ianthe. And only one of them had returned. He didn't think that would happen tonight; he was not so superstitious. It was just…it was difficult not to feel connected to that other time. To that old grief.

He felt a featherlight touch on his cheek, against his ruined skin, followed by the slow, hot press of her lips just by the corner of his mouth. "I'm not afraid of you," she said again. "And everything will be fine tonight. It will."

She moved her hand down his arm, slipping her fingers through his and drawing them down between the two of them. She was holding his hand. Such a simple gesture, and utterly unsexual, and yet, he felt it burn hot inside him.

He imagined that every touch from her would burn hot inside him now.

"It's okay," she said, her voice soft.

He didn't need comfort. But, there was something to be said for it.

It was surprising to him how easy it was to get in the car, how easy it was to go on those winding roads he had been on the night of the accident. All the way to the airport.

Her mouth dropped open slightly when he told her they were going on a private plane to Santa Milagro. "I didn't realize…"

"Well," he said, "we are on an island. You didn't think we were going to drive the whole way, did you?"

"I guess not."

An hour later the wheels on the plane touched down in Santa Milagro, a mountainous country wedged in between Portugal and the Andalusian region of Spain. Sun washed and golden in the day, it glittered tonight. The lights of the city twinkling in the hillside, mirroring the stars that glittered overhead in the velvet blue sky.

When the door to the plane opened, and a limo pulled up to the base of the stairs, Belle's eyes went wide.

"Okay," she said, "this is definitely the most

extravagant arrival I've ever made a party. But then, I'm wearing the most extravagant dress I've ever worn. With the most extravagant man I've ever known."

He looked down at her, smiling slightly. "You think I'm extravagant?"

"A massively muscled prince who looks like he might Hulk out of his suit at any moment? Yes, that is a little bit extravagant."

By the time they got into the car, the similarities between tonight and the night of the accident had begun to fade. He didn't even think about it when he got into the back of the limousine, and Belle took her seat right beside him, her hand still linked with his.

She was comforting him, he realized, which he thought was funny considering this was far more outside her comfort zone than it was out of his. Or, at least, than it would have been only a few years ago. But, he allowed it because he liked the feel of her soft skin against his. Because he enjoyed touching her. And he very much enjoyed her touching him.

"We won't be going back to Olympios tonight," he said casually.

"We won't be?"

They rounded a curve on the road, coming up to a set of wrought iron gates that opened when the car drew near. And then a palace came into view. A thousand times more ostentatious than his own, lit from bottom to top so that the whole place looked as though it were dipped in gold.

"No," he said, "we will be staying here."

"Wow. So… I forgot to ask you. How do you know Prince Felipe? Did you go to prince school together?"

"We did go to school together. But it wasn't prince school."

"Okay. I guess princes just gravitate toward each other?"

"To a degree. But, we do have another friend. And he is not a prince. In fact, Rafe is from a very poor family. He had a benefactor pay for his education. You will meet Prince Felipe and Rafe tonight. And I will introduce you to them as my lover, as well."

"You're even going to lie to your friends?"

"Is it a lie?"

Color bled into her cheeks. "We didn't…that is…we didn't exactly—"

"You did," he said simply, not minding so much that she was clearly embarrassed, because he was unsatisfied, and wasn't that so much worse.

"Perhaps," she bit out. "But we still didn't… all the way."

"That gives us something to look forward to." The car stopped, and the driver got out and opened their door. He extended his hand. "And it gives you something to think about for the evening. Happy thought to hold on to as we make our entrance, as we are about to do. We are going to be announced, and you cannot look angry at me. Rather, you need to look as though you just came from my bed."

Her cheeks were thoroughly flushed after that comment, and by the time they walked up the wide, ornately decorated walkway into the doors that led to the ballroom, he was fairly satisfied that she looked as though he had had his way with her in the car.

Sadly, that was not the case, or his body wouldn't ache as it did.

When they arrived at the top of the stairs, a hush fell over the room.

The herald straightened when they arrived and addressed the crowd. "Presenting Prince Adam Katsaros of Olympios and Belle Chamberlain of California, USA."

She went stiff beside him as they began to walk down the stairs, holding on to him as they moved deeper into the room. Clearly, she wasn't used to being stared at like this. Well, neither was he. Or rather, he was, but this was the first time he had been stared at because he was something less than beautiful.

People looked at him with mouths wide-open, their expressions full of pity, full of shock. And he felt...he felt nothing. He felt strangely in control. As he moved into the room with the most beautiful woman in attendance on his arm, with a strange sense of power rolling over his skin.

People were afraid of him. They had never been afraid of him before. There was something about that that made him feel as though he was in even more control than he had been before. Yes, before people had been his sycophants. Had done everything they could to try to get a favor from him, to get his attention. But now? Now people made way for him as he walked through the room, parting as though they were the sea and he was performing a miracle.

They continued moving through the crowd, making their way to the center of the dance floor. Couples swirled around them, also giving them a wide berth as though he might reach out and grab one of them if they came too close.

"Would you care to dance with me?" he asked.

He looked down at Belle, and he saw that there was no fear in her eyes when she looked back at him. No, she wasn't looking at him like everyone else in the room. She did look terrified. But she was looking at him with a mixture of awe and wonder, and a kind of fascination that he was certain would be his undoing.

"Yes," she said, extending her hand.

He caught it in his own, pulling her toward him. She braced her hand against his chest, pressing her forehead against his shoulder as he swept her up and into the rhythm of the music that filled the room.

People continued to dance around them, though some stopped and stared openly, clearly fascinated by whatever the story might be between the disfigured Prince and the beautiful American who looked at him like a man, and not a curiosity.

And then, all that faded into the background. Years spent in solitude made it preferable in many ways to shut out all the extravagant sensory input that surrounded him. More people than he had seen in any one place in years, more light, more sound.

All of it seemed to go fuzzy around the edges as he looked down at Belle. She consumed him. His vision, his need, his body. Tonight, they would be staying in the palace in Santa Milagro, and most certainly if he asked his friend to provide them with separate bedrooms he would.

Felipe wouldn't even question it. Oftentimes, men in their circumstances had to do things for appearances, and a facade of chastity was not outside the realm of those needs.

But he would not. Because tonight, he was

intent of taking Belle Chamberlain to bed. He could not keep her; he knew that. It was not feasible. But, he could have her for a little while, and he would. *Boyfriends be damned. Decency be damned.*

Her hand was so small in his, so fragile, and while the suit, the surroundings, didn't seem to fit at all, this did. However he had changed over the past three years, however he had come to reform until he no longer fit the position he had been born into, he had been forged into a shape that seemed to fit her just fine.

Her gold dress glittered beneath the lights, but the gown didn't shine more brightly than she did. He thought back to what his adviser had said earlier in his room. About her being the woman who could potentially break the spell of darkness he had been under.

She was light. So, he could see how the other man might think that. But the darkness inside him was the kind that would consume light, not the kind that could be flooded out so simply. The guilt, the pain that he carried with him, would simply leech all that beauty out of her eventually. He would not subject either of them to such a thing.

He had felt one woman die in his arms already; he would not kill this one by inches over the course of years spent in his presence.

But, that did not mean he couldn't satisfy his need for her.

When the song ended, he brought them both to a standstill, lifted her hand to his lips and pressed his mouth against her knuckles. And when he looked around at the people watching them again, their expressions had changed.

Everything was working the way he had intended it to. Because now they saw a man. A man who was with a woman, who was clearly human, and not simply an object to be pitied or feared.

But, for the first time he was concerned about the headline that would be plastered across papers around the world tomorrow. About what they would say concerning Belle. Initially, he hadn't cared if she was hurt, because she had involved herself, because she had come to vouch for her father, in his mind he had imagined it some sort of poetic justice that she become an accessory to his revenge, as well.

Now he wondered.

Her mother was the child of somebody famous. She did have a boyfriend, as she continually pointed out. There would be ramifications for her. The words that would be used to describe a woman who would warm the bed of a man simply because he was powerful, disregarding his looks, would not be kind at all.

He felt a twinge of regret at that. But he could afford nothing else. Nothing deeper. All he could do was make the headline true.

He would push all that to the side for now, and focus on the way she was looking at him. Take everything he could have tonight, because after tonight, when reality hit, when the media had weighed in on the spectacle, it would be different. Things would change.

And she would leave.

He had to let her go after; there was no other choice. Because he certainly couldn't keep her.

He looked around the room again, saw Felipe standing in the back talking to a redhead who was wearing a very brief, very shiny dress. Then, in an isolated corner, he spotted his friend Rafe.

Of course, Rafe would stick to the outer edges of the room. His vision was severely compromised, and though he claimed he could sometimes see light and shadow, Adam wondered how serious it was truly. He had been lost in his own hell for so long that he had left Rafe alone in his.

Adam preferred to be alone in his hell, so part of him assumed that Rafe wanted the same.

"Come," Adam said. "I will introduce you to my friends."

He wasn't certain why he was doing this. Wasn't sure what the point was. But, he found himself crossing the broad expanse of the ballroom, making his way toward Rafe.

"Belle," he said, placing his hand on her lower back, a sign of possessiveness, even if it was one his friend could not observe. "This is Rafael Marelli, but the two friends he has call him Rafe."

Rafe angled his head and looked in Belle's direction, but it was clear that his dark eyes were unseeing. "And the two friends Adam has hardly call him at all," Rafe returned. "It's nice to meet you."

"Belle," she said, extending her hand. "Belle Chamberlain."

Again, seemingly on instinct, Rafe reacted appropriately, lifting his hand slowly until his palm came into contact with hers; then he lowered his head and kissed her knuckles, just as Adam had earlier. Adam felt a surge of rage, possessiveness, overtake him.

"There is no need for that," Rafe said, releasing his hold on her hand, as though he sensed Adam's irritation. "I'm not going to try and steal her from you, Adam. Though, I can see how you would be concerned. Since you have found a woman willing to tame the rather savage beast, she might be a good bet for me, as well."

"Adam." The voice of Prince Felipe came from behind them. Adam turned briefly, and so did Belle. Rafe stayed as he was. "You actually came." His friend assessed him slowly. They hadn't seen each other in years. Not since the scars had healed over. When he had been incapacitated, Felipe had come and seen him, but in the years since he had seemed dedicated to respecting Adam's desire for solitude.

"I said that I would," Adam said, "and I don't pretend I'm going to do something and then sidestep. I tell you how I feel up front—you know me well enough to know that."

"And who is this?" Felipe asked, his sharp eyes turning to Belle.

"Belle," she said, receiving a kiss on the hand from Felipe, as well.

"Adam doesn't like that," Rafe said, his voice dry.

"You're far too perceptive, Rafe," Felipe said. "It's one of the most annoying things about you. You should miss more than you do, God knows."

"Maybe my other senses are heightened."

"You were always like this," Felipe said, waving a hand.

"Is this all you intended it to be?" Adam asked, directing the question at Felipe.

"The party? Yes. Though, my father is unable to attend due to his ill health."

"Somehow, I imagine the citizens of your country are not overly saddened by that," Rafe said.

"Of course not," Felipe said, "but we cannot say that. I am poised to take the throne soon, of course. And I am assuming that the woman on your arm is discreet, Adam, as you are the most discreet man I know."

Belle shifted beside him. "I'm not going to repeat anything I hear tonight," she said, nodding. And Adam believed it. Even though she was the daughter of a paparazzo, he believed it.

He marveled at that for a moment. That he could find that kind of trust in her. That he had found it so effortlessly. It was simply there, and he felt as though he couldn't talk himself out of it even if he wanted to.

"Good," Felipe said. "I know Rafe prefers to be mysterious. He would hate for that aura of disinterest to be compromised in any way."

"There is no compromising what is real," Rafe said.

"I have to circulate," Felipe said.

"Does that mean you're going to try and talk a woman into your bed?" Rafe asked.

Adam was particularly amused by this because Rafe hadn't even been able to see Felipe talking to the redheaded woman earlier. But, regardless, he knew their friend.

"Of course not," Felipe said. "I don't have to try. I will succeed." He turned to go, then paused, regarding Adam closely. "It's not that bad."

Then he walked away. It took Adam a moment to realize he probably meant Adam's face.

Then he looked back at Rafe. Who of course had shown absolutely no shock at the change in Adam's appearance. Rafe had been blinded before the accident.

He remembered what Belle had said, that it was lucky Adam had not lost his sight. Rafe had lost his. Though, he had retained his looks. However, Adam had the feeling that meant next to nothing to his friend, who had emerged from whatever had happened to him changed. And not simply because of the loss of his sight, Adam was certain. There was something else to it. Something deeper.

"It's good you're here, Adam," Rafe said. "If you've changed, I wouldn't know."

His friend's words were so in line with what he had been thinking that he had to laugh. "Of course not. Though, I have been informed that it is not my scars that make me a beast."

"That is true," Belle said, her tone muted.

And he didn't know why, but it struck him uncomfortably, that she seemed to think he was a beast still, when he had hoped that she saw him as a man.

"We will let you return to your brooding," Adam said. "Felipe would say that women like that."

"If they do," Rafe said, lifting his drink to his lips, "I wouldn't know about that either."

Adam took Belle's arm and led her back toward the dance floor, pulling her into his hold. "Are you up for another dance?"

She ignored the question, but moved easily into step with him. "Rafe is blind?" she asked.

He realized that it might not be apparent if you didn't know. Though, it was obvious to Adam, who had known him before, and who had witnessed the change in his demeanor, and mannerisms. "Yes," Adam responded. "Not from birth. Five or six years ago. Something happened and he sustained a head injury, though he is reluctant to give the details. You think I am a private man, but you will find Rafe bests me."

"And Felipe is the easygoing one?"

Adam chuckled at that. "Felipe is nothing but a carefully constructed facade. I would say, without hesitation, that he is perhaps the most private of all of us, and does the very best at hiding it. Which I think is what ensures he stays that way."

"Why did you cut yourself off from your friends? They seem like such good friends," Belle said.

"Sometimes you want to stay wounded," he returned, realizing how true it was the moment the words left his mouth. "You don't want anyone to fix you. I wanted to live in my pain forever. My wife was dead, my son…sometimes all of it hits me so hard it still takes my breath away. And in those moments I don't want anyone there. I don't want anyone to tell me it will be okay. Because how can it be? I almost wanted to feel bleak and hopeless forever because then the enormity of their loss could always be felt. Sometimes it feels good to dwell on the dark things."

She was quiet at that. "I understand." The words

were simply offered, but they did something to him. Just as everything about her seemed to do.

"You agree then," he said, not quite sure why he was pushing the topic. "That I'm a beast inside as well as out?"

"Inside, at least," she said. "You must know that I think...that I am attracted to you." Her cheeks turned pink. "I think I have demonstrated over and over again that I find you somewhat irresistible."

"In spite of all of this?" he asked, indicating his face.

"Perhaps because of it. I can't separate the scars from the man I first met. Yes, I have now seen pictures of you without them, but they aren't you. Not to me."

He pondered that for a moment. "But inside..."

"I didn't say it was a bad thing." She was silent for a moment after that. "There is something about it that I find compelling. I associate passion with a lack of control, and I've always been... I've always hated it. I lived with my mother until I was four. I have small snatches of memory of what it was like to live in her house. I didn't like it. It was so chaotic. Everything was so over the top. But I was also devastated when I had to leave. Because it was the only life I knew. Because she was my mother and she gave me away. And I missed her. I cried for her every night. For the longest time. But, when I stopped crying I got angry. And it's like you said. You want to hold on to those things, to those dark feelings, so that you can make sure you're changed by them. So that you can understand why something happened, so that you can understand those terrible, dark places you were forced into." She looked up at him. "For me, that meant trying to find a way to learn from her lessons, so that I wouldn't do anything like what she did to me to anyone else."

She lifted her hand, allowing her thumb to trace that particularly heavy ridge of scar tissue by his mouth. "You're forcing me to look at passion differently," she continued. "It is that beast inside of you, that wild thing that lets you take whatever you want, that is made entirely of need and not of lies or protection…that's what calls to me. It's what I wish I could find inside of myself."

He reached up, grabbing her wrist, drawing it

to his lips and pressing his mouth to the tender skin there. Neither of his friends had kissed that skin. It was much more intimate. Much more sensitive. And it was all his. She was his. "I could help you find it," he said, his voice rough, his body hardening at the thought.

"Please," she said, the word a whisper. "Please Adam. I want you."

CHAPTER EIGHT

SHE KNEW EXACTLY what she was asking for. But she was tired of pretending it wasn't what she wanted. She had been determined to make it his responsibility. And then, when he had done all those things to her that had made her shake and shiver, that had affected a small earthquake inside her body, she had run away.

Had avoided him as diligently as she possibly could. As if she could wait him out. Until the timer was up on her sentence.

But, she was done with that. Done with it completely. Tonight, she was cocooned in fantasy, at a ball in a beautiful palace with the only prince who would ever rule over her heart. Yes, in the end she would have to sort everything out with Tony, and she was probably being a bad person, giving herself to another man when she had avoided doing that with the man she'd been dating for months.

But for some reason, in Adam's arms everything seemed clear. Desire, need and that hungry thing inside her that might be a beast.

She was so tired of pushing it all down. So tired of pretending to feel nothing, of forcing herself to want nothing. She had clung to that stability she'd been given by her father, to every easy, responsible thing that had come her way, because she had been certain it would be the key to protecting herself from further injury. The key to protecting herself from hurting other people. And here she was, considering doing something that would certainly hurt at least one person.

That made her stomach seize up tight. But, it was something she would have to deal with later. If she had a phone on her, she would deal with it now, but she had been prevented from making any contact with the outside world, so she couldn't. And anyway, it was probably for the best. That she was cut off from all that safety, from that familiarity.

In many ways, being taken captive by Adam

had led to a strange kind of freedom. She wasn't beholden to anyone. Didn't have to be the perfect daughter, didn't have to be an example of anything. She was cut off completely from all her responsibility, from everyone who knew her. Everyone who knew her as Belle Chamberlain, the very levelheaded, bookish girl who led with her head and never her heart. And certainly never the needs of her body.

None of those people were here to judge her. None of those people were here for her to please or impress. And without that…

She wanted him. And she would have him.

"Adam," she said, his name a plea on her lips. "When do we get to leave the party?"

He growled, drawing her up against him, his arm like a steel band around her waist. "Now," he said, that voice shot through with iron just like the rest of him.

She found him leading her off the dance floor, out of the ballroom. "Where are we going?" she asked.

"I assume that Felipe readied the room I normally stay in when I come to visit."

"Oh. Did you often stay here? With—"

"No," he said quickly. "We never stayed here together. This is not about her. This is not about recapturing some kind of memory, or stepping into the past. I can promise you that. My marriage is entirely separate from this. I swear to you."

A wave of relief washed over her. She didn't know why it mattered. It shouldn't. This wasn't about emotion; it wasn't about love. Yes, Adam had tapped into something inside of her, had captured a part of her that no one else ever had before. Awakened it. But, she didn't need to compete with his wife. Adam had loved his wife; she could see it in that expression of pure happiness on his face in the photograph in his room. He'd had a future set before him, a hope and joy that had been ripped from him. She could never presume to understand it. Would never ask that he relinquish any kind of hold on it.

She didn't want him to push his wife out of his heart. She simply wanted a space with him for now. That was all.

She knew that people were looking at them,

that guests and staff members alike were regarding them with curiosity as they made their hasty exit.

Adam paused for a moment, reaching into his pocket as his phone buzzed. "A text from Felipe, who has indeed informed me that my room is prepared. And confirmed the location. Clearly, he was paying attention."

"A good friend to have," she said, her voice sounding thin even to her own ears.

She wondered if she should tell him now. About her inexperience. But, she didn't want to do anything to compromise what had grown between them. And that meant changing any perception he might have of her. It was too late. They could have a postmortem after, because she doubted she would be able to affect the role of experienced woman with any kind of skill. She would wait until after.

He was so large and sure beside her, and she gloricd in that strength as he took the lead, sweeping them both through the halls effortlessly. His confidence, his certainty, filled her with her own.

There was something about his strength that

made her eminently conscious of how delicate she was, and yet made her feel all the stronger for it. It was some kind of magic. That she could feel small, fragile and yet also as though she held this large, impossible, impenetrable man in the palm of her hand. That she had the power to affect him. That she had power in this situation at all.

If it was a dream, she didn't want to wake up from it. If it was fantasy, she was in no hurry to get back to reality.

Finally, they arrived at a set of ornate red doors that she knew led to the bedchamber. Her heart slammed up, seeming to hit her at the base of her throat, making it impossible to breathe.

Adam must have noticed the sudden fit of nerves. Because he reached out, smoothing her lower lip with his thumb. "You have nothing to fear from me. I want… I want this," he said, his voice growing frayed. Raw. "I was going to give you some kind of speech. Beautiful words. Something seductive, I suppose. But I am out of practice. And all I can offer you is honesty. I want to lose myself in you. I have spent years wandering through the darkness, losing myself

there. And you…you are light to me, Belle. I want
to lose myself in that, if only for a little while. I
know that it can't be more than a night. I know
that after this I must let you go, as I have prom-
ised. But, just for a while. I want to be lost in
something beautiful. And you are the most beautiful thing I have ever seen. I may have seen
beauty before my accident, before my loss, but I
didn't see it the way that I do now. It could never
have meant as much to me then. After so many
years of ugliness, so many years of solitude. So
many years of darkness. You cannot know what
it means to have you touch me." He cupped her
cheek, his hand large, rough, his expression ear-
nest. "I don't know how many women I've been
with. I never bothered to count. For years, there
was only my wife, but before that… I was a
prince, I was young and handsome and powerful and I made the most of that. It doesn't matter.
Because a single touch from you, your fingertips
on my face as it is now erases all of that. It is so
much heavier—it has so much more value. Now,
as the man I am today, it is without price. I am
not a man given to speeches. I'm not a man given

to emotion. But I am full with both now. And I want you to know that. You are not my prisoner. I have grown to suspect that I might be yours."

Those words washed over her, threw her, warming her, making her feel a flood of that earlier certainty, that earlier strength. Yes, this was the man she wanted. This was the moment. Because it meant everything. Because it wasn't simply about being carried away on a tide of passion. It was a decision, a need, given in to with the full cost clear to her.

Because it would rattle the fabric of the life she had left behind, because it would change the situation Adam had been living in for the past three years. Because both of them would leave it marked as indelibly as Adam had been by his accident.

That was what she wanted. That was what she craved. To have this chance to affect someone's life so profoundly. To affect her own so deeply.

When she had been removed from her mother's care, she didn't think the woman had lost a moment of sleep over it. In fact, she had likely thrown a party. She had managed to make no change in the life of her own mother, and that wounded her deeper and more profoundly than she had ever realized before this moment.

But Adam would remember her. He would think of her. No matter who came after her, she would always be the first woman to touch him after he had been so changed. After he had been scarred. She would always be the first woman he had chosen.

Dear God, how she craved this. How she hungered for being chosen.

So, she stretched up on her toes and kissed him, lost herself in him, in this. Poured out everything inside her that he seemed to think was light, and committed herself to giving her all. To giving all of herself.

When they parted, they were both breathing heavily, her heart fluttering in her chest like a bird trapped in a cage. "Please," she said, not caring if she was begging. "I know that you want whatever you see in me, the light, the beauty. But I want everything inside of you." She put her hand flat on his chest, felt his heartbeat rage beneath her palm. "I don't need you to change. I don't want you to. I don't want you to stop being a beast. I want you to show me how to be one too."

"I can do that." He pushed open the doors, drawing her into his arms and propelling them both into the room. Then he closed the door firmly behind them, leaving them shrouded in darkness, shrouded in privacy. She thought for a moment that he might leave the lights extinguished. But he did not. Instead, he flicked the switch, bathing them in light. Leaving no chance to hide from this moment. From what they felt. From what they were about to do.

It made it all the more terrifying, certainly, but it also made it feel more real. More stark. She wouldn't be able to block it out in the misty haze of darkness, and she found herself grateful for it.

Because if this was her big, loud moment, she should allow nothing to temper it. Nothing at all.

"I want… I want to see you," she said, the words coming out with a bit more of a stutter than she would have liked. But, she was a virgin, after all, and the confidence that she was clinging to was tenuous at best.

A strange expression crossed his face. "I had

not thought anyone ever would again. Not as I am now."

He undid the knot that held his bow tie to his throat, then cast the strip of black fabric onto the floor. He began to undo the buttons of his shirt, exposing a glorious wedge of tanned, toned chest as he did.

She was held captive by him, by that sheer masculine beauty.

She saw shirtless men at the beach all the time, and given that it was Southern California, a lot of them had that perfect gym-sculpted look. But, most of them were waxed within an inch of their lives, leaving behind none of the glorious, masculine chest hair that graced Adam's body.

As he let his shirt fall to the ground with his tie, revealing a sculpted, toned body that spoke of his physical strength, she found herself mourning that current trend of minimizing a man's testosterone.

She loved it. She loved how feral it was. How untamed. But then, given the fact that she loved that this man was a beast, it didn't surprise her that she felt that way.

"The rest," she said, her throat growing tight.

He kept his dark eyes fixed on hers as he reached down, working the belt free, then undoing the closure on his pants, as well. He pushed the pants and underwear down in one motion, leaving him gloriously naked for her appraisal.

She had never seen a naked, aroused man in the flesh, and nothing had prepared her for the sight of Prince Adam Katsaros in all his glory.

Truly, she hadn't known men could be quite so large. Or quite so hard. And that wasn't just the most intimate part of him, but all of him. He looked as though he were fashioned from the rock, life breathed into him by some kind of mythical creature. And since she felt as though she were lost in a fairy tale, that didn't seem fanciful at all.

"What is it?" he asked, his voice surprisingly gentle given the brutally masculine sight he affected before her.

"You're just...*beautiful* seems an insipid word," she said. "And nothing about you is insipid. But you take my breath away—that much I know."

"I'm not sure I'm worthy of such compliments.

However, I am happy as long as you are happy. And as long as I can entice you to reveal your beauty to me."

She reached behind her back clumsily, her fingers shaking as she felt for the zipper on her dress. She wanted to do this. For him. Wanted to be the first woman that he saw naked after all these years. But, she had a hard time, the tiny zipper catching itself on the folds of fabric and sequins. "I'm nervous," she said.

A smile curved his lips, lips she could never think of as ruined again. And his smile…she could never think of it as compromise. It was his. And she could see it now, could easily read it, regardless of whether or not anyone else would ever be able to recognize it in quite the same way she did.

"Let me," he said, that gentle tone combined with the firm touch of his hands at her hips putting her instantly at ease.

He dealt with her zipper deftly, her dress falling loose at her waist, then to the floor, a golden pool around her feet.

She was left in nothing more than a pair of

whisper-thin underwear. Her dress didn't require a bra, so her breasts were bare to him.

He had already touched her there, had already put his hands on her intimately, and she found she wasn't embarrassed in the least.

Especially not when he clenched his jaw tight, the obvious restraint it was taking for him to hold himself back speaking to how deeply she affected him.

She liked that. Gloried in the fact that she tested him. It did make her wonder about Tony. No, she would not have liked him to pressure her, but that was something separate entirely. He didn't look at her like this. Didn't look at her with all this naked need, with this barely repressed desire.

Maybe if he had, she would have wanted him.

Except, she knew that wasn't true. Knew that part of herself had always been waiting for Adam. Even before she had known who he was.

He surprised her by dropping to his knees, pressing a kiss to the tender skin beneath her belly button before grabbing hold of her panties and dragging them down her thighs. He was eye level with the most intimate part of her then, and that made her feel exposed. Naked, when before she hadn't felt that way.

"Adam—" Her words were cut off as he leaned forward, pressing his face to her inner thigh and inhaling deeply, the rough, sandpaper quality of his evening stubble on the fragile skin there sending a shiver of pleasure up her spine.

Then he turned to her, tasting her deeply right where she ached for him most. She stiffened, and arched back, and his hand clamped down hard on her lower back before sliding down to cup her rear, drawing her back forward, holding her to his mouth as he subjected her to a sensual assault that far surpassed anything she had imagined possible.

He wasn't Prince Charming. Wasn't the soft, smooth fantasy man she had always imagined she might end up with. But then, she imagined Prince Charming would never think of doing something quite like this.

The intensity of his desire was evident with each pass of his tongue, and when he brought his hands in—stroking her, teasing her—she lost her mind completely. Lost the ability to analyze anything that was happening. She simply gave herself up to sensation. To him.

To passion. She didn't feel so afraid of it now, not when it had consumed her so beautifully, not when he consumed her so beautifully.

Her orgasm washed over her like a wave, different from that time in the library, where it had felt so fraught and fractured. This time, it was warm and comforting, rolling through her with building intensity, going on and on and leaving her gasping for air.

He rose up slowly, kissing her stomach, her rib cage just beneath her breast and then her lips. He kept one palm cupping her butt, the hold possessive, a demonstration of strength that made her knees weak. He pulled her naked body up against his, let her feel that hot, hard length that clearly proved his desire for her.

He pushed his fingers through her hair, pulling her hard into the kiss. She felt wrapped in him, consumed by him, his scent, his heat, the strength and hardness of his body, and when he walked them both to the bed she didn't feel afraid. She didn't feel nervous; she didn't feel

unsure. This was Adam, and she wanted him.
Whatever that might mean, whether it might hurt,
or whether it might leave her heart feeling torn
after…it didn't matter. At least, it didn't outweigh
the overwhelming need she felt to be joined to
him in this way.

Adam lowered her slowly onto the plush mattress, gripping her thigh, moving his hand down
behind her knee, teasing the sensitive skin there
as he lifted her leg slowly, draping it over his
lower back, moving himself into position between her spread legs.

He flexed his hips forward, sliding that thick
arousal through her slick folds, making her gasp,
building her arousal back up, impossibly, perfectly, to the heights it was just before her last
climax.

She reached up, grabbing his face, holding him
steady, looking in his eyes as she rocked her hips
against him, in time with his movements, making
them both gasp. He moved to the side, and she
tried to stop him, bereft as the cold air washed
over her when he removed himself.

"What?"

"If I know Felipe…" He opened up a drawer on a nightstand next to the bed and produced a box. "Yes," he said, "I do."

They were condoms. He opened them, taking out the plastic packet and tearing it quickly before rolling the protection over his length. She watched, fascinated, because she had never seen it done before, because she was fascinated by everything about him. By the strength in his hand as he gripped his own shaft and smoothed the latex over himself.

Then he was right back where he had been only a moment ago, positioned at the entrance to her body, one hand gripping her thigh, another pressed into the mattress by her face. He lifted her gently, the blunt head of his arousal pressing more firmly against her as he did.

A slow, intense stinging sensation began to build, burn as he moved deeper inside her, joining their bodies together, filling her, stretching her. She gritted her teeth, screwed her eyes shut tight, bringing her hands back above her head and balling them into fists, her nails digging into her palms as she did her best not to show him her distress.

He flexed his hips forward an inch more, and she gasped, her eyes flying open wide. But he wasn't looking at her. His unfocused gaze was somewhere behind her, his jaw held tight, the chords in his neck standing, demonstrating how hard-won his control was.

Something about that made her heart clench tight, made the pain begin to recede. Watching him, watching how profoundly it affected him, how deeply he felt it. She focused on that, she focused on him, and, as he slid in deeper, she felt herself expand to accommodate him, felt it grow easier to take him, felt her desire to take him build.

He growled, thrusting inside her to the hilt, tightening his hold on her thigh and drawing her up hard against him. It took her breath away, overwhelmed her. For a moment, she didn't think she could possibly endure it. Didn't think she could possibly withstand it.

When he began to move, it was intense, it was rough and it was raw. She could see that this

was different from everything else that had occurred before. That had all been about giving
to her, giving her pleasure. In this moment, he
was claiming his own. Was expending the years
of frustration, loneliness, pain in her body. Was
using her to find his own release. And somehow,
that gave her strength.

She wanted to be this for him. Wanted to be
all that he needed, because nobody else could
be, and nobody else would be. Because he had
asked no one else. Because he said he wanted no
one else.

She clung to his shoulders, met his each and
every thrust, and as she did, as she gave herself over to this, over to him, all the discomfort
faded. Or maybe it didn't fade; perhaps it simply
blended into the growing pleasure that bloomed
in her midsection and spread outward, taking
root deep inside her and made it so she couldn't
think, couldn't breathe.

There was nothing but him. But the rough feel
of his whiskers against her cheek, then the slick
slide of his tongue against hers. The scent of his

body, masculine and spicy, his hardness over her, inside her. Everything was Adam.

She had never felt like his captive, not fully. She had never acted like a prisoner, had never given him the proper deference, as he had been the first to point out. But now...she felt fully taken captive. Utterly and completely.

He was rough; he was demanding; he was everything. She did her best to meet it, did her best to soften when he needed her to soften, to return force when he required it. When his teeth scraped along the edge of her lip, she returned the favor with a bite of her own and was rewarded with a low, feral growl.

Pleasure built inside her, blending in with the luxurious feel of the bedspread beneath her, and the hot weight of Adam above her.

She felt it when his control began to fray, and she lifted her hands, gripping his face, tracing that thick scar tissue that created a map of his pain across his skin. And when he shuddered, gave himself up to his own release, something deep and dark began to pulse inside her.

Her release hit when his did, and there was

something different about this one too. It wrapped around them both, held them both in thrall; they shook together, clung to each other as the storm took them both over.

He moved his hands to her face, held on to her tightly and pressed his forehead against hers, then closed the distance between their lips and claimed her mouth in a kiss. One that mimicked everything that had just happened between them.

And then he pulled her against the side of his body, cradling her against him, his breath hot on her cheek, his large hand splayed possessively over her stomach.

She had thought they might talk. About her inexperience. About what had happened. About what came next.

She realized they couldn't talk about any of it, not without addressing the *next*. And she didn't want to. She wanted to stay here. In the moment. With nothing behind her and nothing in front of her. In this moment, in this night, where she could be as free as she wanted.

Where she could hide with him. Glory in him. So she didn't speak at all. Instead, she turned her face to his and kissed him, a hand pressed lightly to his shoulder.

It was all he needed. He consumed her lips on a growl, and they both let themselves get caught up in passion again.

CHAPTER NINE

HE WANTED TO keep her prisoner forever. That was the thought running through Adam's head the next morning, all the way back to the airport, on the flight that took them back to Olympios.

Belle was intoxicating. Being with her was being able to touch the light again, if for just moments at a time. His beautiful, innocent captive who had never been with a man before he'd been with her.

He had known after. In the middle of all of it there had been no thought, and he'd had no ability to process what the tension in her body, that slight resistance as he'd slid deep inside her, had meant.

He supposed it should make him feel guilty. The fact that he—the man who'd taken her prisoner, who had left her with so few choices—should be the first to have her.

But he was a man capable of taking her prisoner, so guilt wouldn't be coming to the party anytime soon. No, instead he felt replete with a kind of bone-deep satisfaction he couldn't recall feeling before.

But it would fade. Later today when he sent her back home to California on his jet, it would fade.

He had to let her go. He had no other choice.

He had done it. He had gone out in public, and what the world would think of it remained to be seen, but he also didn't want it.

He didn't want Belle's suffering. He didn't want revenge. Not on her, not on her father. Whatever rage he felt over Ianthe's death—over his son's death—it was still real. But they couldn't be brought back, no matter who he punished. If he took the photographer who had caused the accident prisoner, locked him away for the rest of his life, Ianthe would still be dead. His future, his heart, would still be gone.

And in his quest to rectify something that could never truly be repaired, he would destroy that one beautiful, light thing that still remained in this world. Belle. He could not. And he would not.

She had been subdued during the plane ride, and was growing even more so on the car ride back to the palace. She knew; she knew that this was coming to an end. The fact that she seemed upset about it only drove home the point that it was the right thing to do.

The fact that she had begun to feel sorry for him, the fact that she felt some sort of connection with him, was probably the most despicable part of all of it. If she would think of him ever after this, if she would miss him, want him, when he could never be a man worthy of those things...then he had truly created an environment wherein he could never fully release her.

Part of him reveled in that, because he was only a man. Enjoyed the idea that somewhere, someone would think of him. Would miss him. Would want him.

But he didn't want it to be her. He wanted her

to go back to her boyfriend. To enjoy that bright California sunshine and all the security and freedom she had spoken of when she talked of her home.

He didn't want her here. In the darkness with him.

She had told him she wanted to learn how to be a beast, wanted to learn how to embrace her passion. And if he had managed to help her with that, if she could only carry that back with her, if it made her happier, if it made her life better, then that was a good thing.

The alternative was something he didn't want to consider. That he had infected her with his darkness, and that over the course of the next few years it would continue to spread inside her until she matched him. If his darkness was so strong that it had blotted out her light, he didn't suppose he could ever forgive himself.

Have you ever forgiven yourself for anything? For your wife? For your son? What does this add? Nothing.

He shrugged that off, but as they approached the gates of the palace he saw something that sent a shock of adrenaline down his spine. Immediately, he was on alert, ready to fight, ready to defend the woman at his side. Because there were people surrounding the palace, people with cameras, microphones, video equipment. There were vans; there was a damned helicopter circling overhead. They had come back to a circus.

"What is this?" he asked no one in particular, because he knew that Belle didn't have the answer either.

The limousine slowed, his driver clearly hesitant to go on. Adam pushed the button that lowered the divider. "Can you drive through them?" he asked.

"I'm sure that if I continue to drive, they'll move eventually," the driver said.

"Test that," Adam returned, his voice hard.

"What's going on?"

"You should know well," Adam said, pulling his phone out of his pocket and opening up the web browser. "It's the paparazzi."

"I didn't talk to anybody," she said, her voice shaking. "I didn't."

"I know that," he said. "You were with me the

entire night, remember? And not only that, but last night we made our public debut. So this is hardly a complete shock. Though, I have to confess I didn't think this would be the result." There had to be something else. Something more. Yes, there were a great many headlines talking about his first appearance in the public eye since his accident had occurred, but that wasn't enough to cause this kind of frenzy. Not when there were already photographs. There was nothing new to be gained...unless...

He pulled up a headline for an American newspaper, and that was when he saw it. "What is your boyfriend's name?"

"Tony," she said. "Tony Layton."

"Yes, he is not happy. And that is why these people are here."

"What?"

He handed her his phone; there was no point keeping it from her. If she wanted to dial her father or her boyfriend, or the National Guard, she was welcome to do so. He'd been invaded already, and she was already set to go. So what did it matter?

Her mouth fell open, her eyes widening with shock as she looked down at the screen. "He's claiming that you've kidnapped me. That I'm brainwashed. Stockholm syndrome." She put the phone down, meeting his gaze. Then she reached out, pressing the button that divided them from the driver. "Stop the car," she commanded.

The driver did so, mostly out of shock, Adam imagined. He was about to open his mouth to contradict Belle, but the car had stopped and she was already getting out the passenger-side door.

"Hey! Do you want to listen to a third party, or do you want to hear the story from me? I am not Prince Adam Katsaros's prisoner. I am his fiancée. I have chosen to be here with him. I'm in love with him, and we are going to get married."

Belle was completely numb with shock, unable to believe the words that had just come out of her mouth. She had claimed to be Adam's fiancée. Had claimed they were getting married. When she had seen Tony's words in bold in the news article she had lost her mind completely. This was passion, she supposed. That total insanity she had feared for most of her life. Had feared would overtake her completely. And it had.

She couldn't regret it, though. As she stood there, facing down the horde of paparazzi, that was the thing that surprised her the most. That she wasn't filled with remorse or regret. That she wasn't beset by fear. She had always imagined that she would be horrified if she were ever to give in to such impulses. That she would hate all the changes in herself. That she would feel like she had failed in some way.

But, that wasn't the case. She felt…everything felt clear. Quiet. Everything felt like it was moving in slow motion. Which could indicate that she was in shock rather than having a moment of clarity, but she liked the clarity idea better.

Somehow, over the course of the past weeks, she had been made into the person she was always supposed to become. In Adam's arms, in Adam's bed she had found a part of herself that she had kept suppressed for a long time. Had found a part of herself she hadn't known she needed to find.

Now that she had…she felt more full, more whole than she ever had.

She felt brave. She realized that was the biggest difference. Yes, it had taken a great amount of bravery to come here and free her father, and that had been something of an out-of-body experience. Something beyond her typical capacity for strength.

It had felt foreign then. Strange.

This felt like part of herself. Like it was the most instinctual, easy thing in all the world to defend Adam, to defend the man she had fallen in love with.

Even that realization didn't scare her. Even if it should. It felt as calm and clear as everything else. Of course she loved him. That was why this was simple. That was why there was no other option.

She was not going to allow a torch-carrying mob to accuse him of being a monster. Was not going to allow reporters, the media, to invade the sanctuary that he had ensconced himself in for so long. Not when they were the ones who had caused all his pain.

She wouldn't allow it. She couldn't.

The roar that came from the reporters when she made her revelation was almost deafening, cutting through that sense of calm she had felt only a moment before. But, it didn't penetrate. Not deeply. She was still sure of her course.

"Do you want to listen? Or do you want to make wild guesses about what the truth might be? I can tell you everything," she said. And even though she was pretty sure they hadn't been able to hear the exact words she had spoken, they did quiet down.

"I was not kidnapped. I have not been tricked, and I have not been manipulated. Prince Adam Katsaros is not forcing my hand in any way. In fact, he was going to allow me to return home to avoid damaging my reputation. But I refused. I am refusing," she reiterated. She looked back at the car, saw Adam sitting inside, staring out at her, his expression fierce.

"How dare you go after a man who has already been through so much," she said, her voice trembling. "How dare you believe these lies?"

"Yes," one of the reporters in the back of the

crowd spoke loudly. "But you can't blame the public for being suspicious. Beauty might love the beast in a fairy tale, but not in real life."

Rage spiked through her. "You will find that there are a great many women who prefer a beast," she said, her words crisp. "Prince Charming might be a good dancer, but a beast has other qualities to recommend him."

She knew that was going to land her a very salacious write-up. But she didn't care. It was true. He was the one she wanted, him and no one else.

Then Adam got out of the car, slowly. He was so large, his presence so vital, so intimidating, that she felt the reporters shrink back.

"I think what my fiancée is trying to say," he said, his deep, rich voice rolling over her skin, sending little tremors through her body, "is that we have a particular connection. If it doesn't make for a clever headline for you, I can't say that I'm particularly sorry. But it is time for me to move on, time for my country to move on, from the tragedy that was caused at the hands of this kind of overzealous media. Your responsibility is to report on world events, events that would inform or protect the public. Last I checked, who might be sharing my bed is not one of those events. You may show yourselves off the palace grounds and out of my country, or you will find yourself thrown in prison. And if you think I'm exaggerating, there is a photographer I can put you in contact with who will let you know that I never bluff." He looked across the car, his eyes meeting hers. "Come, *agape*—we should go home now."

That was easy enough that Belle knew he was not going to be quite so biddable when they were alone. But still, she found herself obeying his command. Following his lead and getting back into the car.

"Drive," he commanded, and the car began to move again.

"I couldn't let that headline stand," she said, justifying herself before he even said a word.

"Neither could I," he responded. "Though, I'm not certain your solution would have been mine."

"You can always retract it later. Engagements break up all the time."

He turned to face her, his dark eyes blazing. "Is that what you were hoping for?"

She shook her head. "No. Actually, I wasn't. When I said those words it was with the full intention of marrying you. Becoming your wife in every sense of the word. After what we shared together last night... I was never going to go back to Tony. And, I'm not sure what the hell he was thinking making an announcement like this. Yes, I did need to call him and break up with him. But, since you wouldn't give me a phone, that's hardly my fault."

Something shiny and black hit her lap. And she realized that Adam had flung his phone to her. She shot him a bland stare. "Thank you. But, this might have been helpful last night."

She picked it up, and with shaking fingers dialed Tony's number. He answered on the second ring. "If you have any more questions for me, I will be doing a press conference this evening," he said, his voice much harder and more authoritative than she was accustomed to hearing.

"Tony," she said, "it's me."

"Belle?" He sounded…not exactly relieved. "Why didn't you call me before?"

Adam was glaring at the phone, a murderous glint in his eye. She put the phone away from her ear and turned the speaker on so that Adam could listen in, since she had a feeling he would leap across the car otherwise.

"I didn't have a phone before," she said. "But I do now. I'm nobody's prisoner. Please stop telling the press that Adam is a criminal of some kind. He's not. He's kind, and he's been through so much."

"So, you're saying that you left me of your own free will, and didn't tell myself or your father where you were, and that you presumably cheated on me during that time? After claiming that you were waiting for some kind of magic connection." He made a scoffing sound. "I didn't touch you the entire eight months we dated, and now you're sharing a bed with this monster?"

"He's not a monster, Tony," she insisted. "And I'm sorry. But the only crime committed was mine. I wasn't faithful to you, but I also never intended to come back home to you. Before I ever touched Adam I realized that things needed to be over between us. And the order that I did things in could have been changed. But the result is the same nonetheless. I'm marrying Adam."

"You're *marrying* him?" Tony's voice was incredulous, filled with disgust. "You refused to allow me to share your bed for eight months—you wasted my time making me believe that someday I could gain access to your body if I paid my dues, and then you spread your legs for him immediately, simply because he could offer you a castle? Because he could give you money? I'm sorry, seeing as you were a virgin, Belle, I had no idea you were such a whore."

Suddenly, the telephone was wrenched from her hand.

"I would watch what I said about my fiancée," Adam said. "Belle is going to be a princess, and her husband possesses no small amount of power. I will not hesitate to bring the full weight of that power down upon you if you persist in speaking of her this way."

"Hey," Tony said. "I'm an American, and I

don't have to take anything from you. I have free speech."

"Yes," Adam countered, "and we'll see how well that free speech serves you once no one will do business with you. Because, as you say, the United States is a free country, and with full information people are allowed to make their own decisions. If they decide not to associate with you because of a few well-placed words on my end, well, that is freedom and action, is it not?"

"You bastard," Tony countered. "I'm not going to let you intimidate me. I'm going to keep talking. By the time I'm through with you, everybody will understand that you brainwashed her. She wouldn't even let me get to second base, and now she's banging you? I don't believe it. I'm going to expose you for what you are. Some kind of animal who traps women and then convinces them that the money that you offer is somehow worth the price of getting naked with somebody that messed up."

"Go to hell," Belle hissed, hitting the end button on the phone. She looked up at Adam, her expression fierce. "I'm sorry about that. Unfortunately threats about impacting his business prospects probably won't hurt him. He's a lit major like me. He was willing to accept a lifetime of poverty, and he's much more likely to escape it by tattling to the press."

Adam laughed. "Do you imagine he hurt my feelings? I'm not that easily wounded. However, he might make himself a problem."

"That's why we have to get married," she insisted. "It's the only way to keep everybody from beating down the palace doors."

"Make no mistake—a royal wedding creates its own kind of furor. However, it would be nice to be dealing with that sort of headline rather than an angry mob."

"He had no right," she said.

Adam leaned forward, taking hold of her chin. "He had *every* right. If a man carried you away from me, kept you from me, I would destroy him without mercy, without remorse. As I just proved when your boyfriend said those things about you."

"I think it's safe to say that Tony isn't my boyfriend anymore."

"I suppose he's not." He released his hold on her. "Still, I can't say that I blame him. Though, I am curious. Why did you make him wait? What was it about me that made you decide it was time to be with a man?"

She lifted a shoulder, gazing out the window at the palace. "I told myself all kinds of things. About passion, and about fear. And, maybe some of it's true. I told myself I didn't want to be like my mother. That I wanted to be more selective. That I wanted to make sure I was ready for a stable life, children, marriage, if I was going to get into having sex. But, the bottom line is that I didn't want him. I would have had to put aside a lot of doubt to sleep with him. I would have had to…work to bring myself to the point where I felt I could. With you, I found myself fighting the need to. It was entirely different. It took no restraint to resist him."

His gaze was like molten fire, and she felt her cheeks heating beneath his stare. "I don't care about the scars," she continued. "Or maybe… maybe that isn't even it. Maybe it's just that I find them beautiful. It's difficult to say that, because

I know they represent so much suffering. But, all of that is part of you. And I… I'm happy to marry you, Adam," she said, not quite possessing the bravery to tell him that she loved him. Not just yet.

"I'm not certain I can say I'm happy to get married," he said, his voice rough. "But I am more than happy to share my bed with you."

Those words should have diminished the moment, should have made her feel reduced, badly, she supposed. But, instead, she felt them hit her with the full weight of marriage vows. Adam, who had spent the past three years alone, was happy to share his bed with her.

Maybe it wasn't a confession of love, but it was something. It was something she was going to take, hold close and view as a little bit of hope. Hope that someday, the beast might learn to love her in return.

CHAPTER TEN

BELLE'S ANNOUNCEMENT TO the press was hardly the end of the speculation. Headlines exploded across newspapers around the world. Not just tabloids—but reputable news sources—speculating on the nature of his relationship with this unknown woman from California.

Adam didn't particularly care for all the attention. But, ensconced in the palace it was easy to pretend it wasn't happening.

Or, perhaps more honestly, ensconced in Belle's arms.

It was easy to forget the rest of the world when he was in bed with her. If the entire kingdom had burned down beyond the palace walls, he would not have noticed.

Of course, Belle's transition from prisoner to fiancée had meant making some changes. He had begun to sleep in her bedroom every night. Additionally, he had provided her with a phone, a computer, everything she needed to make contact with the outside world. She had chosen to stay with him, and that meant there was no reason to keep her cut off. In fact, doing so would only prove him the monster the world seemed determined to believe that he was.

He took a sip of coffee and looked down at the newspaper sitting on the top of the stack. The one proclaiming his general monstrosity the loudest. He had to wonder if it wasn't true.

In many ways, all that he was accused of doing was true. Except for the part about him forcing himself on her. Except for the fact that she had chosen to stay with him. That she was the one who had jumped out of the car and announced an engagement the two of them had never discussed.

He had been set to free her. And, yes, they had never discussed that in detail, but he was certain she had been aware of the fact. He had said that after their debut he would concoct a story about the breakup. She had to have known.

Discomfort lodged itself in his chest.

And, even more darkly, he wondered if what

they were saying was true. Stockholm syndrome. That she was only identifying with the person who had taken her captive because of some complex psychological break she had undergone at his hands.

Regardless, he was unwilling to do much about it.

This, while not in his plans, was ideal.

The media was fascinated by Belle, and the fairy tale that would be constructed out of the two of them finding love after tragedy would be a triumphant one indeed.

In fact, he had a ring in his pocket, and he was prepared to make sure that she was bound to him as publicly and permanently as possible. So, all these ruminations on his end were just that. They were never going to turn into anything more.

He was unwilling to do the right thing, if the right thing meant releasing her.

In her arms he had found something next to salvation, and he was determined to hold on to it.

When she walked through the wide doorway and into the dining room his heart constricted. She was—unquestionably—beautiful. He could see why everyone, from the media to the public, doubted why she had chosen to be with him.

A strange thing, to be in this position. He and his late wife had been considered a perfect match in every way. And now he was with a commoner and she was considered his superior. It didn't wound him, but it did make him wonder. What exactly she saw in him, and why.

There was nothing inside him that was superior to any man. Sure, he owned the palace, and he imagined that gave him some sort of advantage. But he could not imagine Belle being that manipulative. Could not imagine that sort of thing mattering to her.

She was happiest curled up in a corner with a book. And she could do that in a tiny cottage as easily as she could in a castle.

She saw something in him…and for the life of him he himself could not see it.

"Good morning," she said, somewhat subdued.

She was wearing a simple sundress that conformed to her curves in a casual way. The soft fabric skimmed her shape in a delicate fashion. The skirt fell well past her knee, swishing with each step. It shouldn't be erotic. It should be sweet if anything. And yet, he felt himself respond to it with a hunger that shocked him. Every time he saw her he felt as though he were in the midst of a long sexual drought. When, in reality, he had had her only a few hours earlier.

Perhaps it was simply the result of those years of celibacy. But, he doubted it.

"Is everything all right?"

She scrubbed her eyes. "I was up early talking to my father. He's, of course, very concerned about the situation. And, about the part he might have played in it."

"In all honesty, he played quite a large part in it. Without him, we would not be here—is that not so?"

She shot him an exasperated look that he couldn't quite figure out whether or not he deserved. "I suppose you could make that argument, Adam, but I don't want to. I don't want my father to feel as though he is somehow at fault for my engagement."

"Does there have to be a guilty party in an

engagement?" He feared that with theirs there might be.

"No," she said, taking a seat a few chairs away from him. She was clearly agitated. And some of it was obviously directed at him.

He had been married to Ianthe for nearly three years, so he was familiar enough with women glaring angrily at him from across the table. Still, with Belle it surprised him. In part because he had committed a vast variety of sins against her, and she had been surprisingly docile about a great many of them but was now looking furiously in his direction only a few hours after he had given her a substantial amount of pleasure. And since then, had had no interaction with her.

One thing had not changed during his seclusion, it appeared. Women were inscrutable.

"Would you like some coffee?"

She sighed. "Do I ever not want coffee?"

"Not in my experience," he said, taking hold of the carafe and pouring her a cup, sliding it in her direction. "But, in my experience you are also not usually so prickly for no reason. Typically, I have to take you captive to earn this level of ire."

"It was just difficult, that's all. Talking to my father and trying to explain the situation."

"And the headlines?"

She looked away. "It's strange. Being the subject of so much scrutiny. I don't like it. And, this is kind of proving your point about the media, and challenging a lot of my perceptions about my upbringing. All in all it's been a little bit of a confronting couple of days."

"I don't suppose people are ever really capable of lingering over the trials of others. They possess too many of their own. Why should the public—struggling financially, working hard to make ends meet—concern themselves with the fate of the rich and famous? With their privacy. There is pain that wealth and status can't erase, but when you are struggling with more, why should you take that on board? Similarly, people in my position are not spared pain. And when it happens, it feels as real as it does for anyone else."

She nodded slowly. "I suppose so. But this is horribly…invasive. And I think that it's cruel. It makes me want to hold a press conference and detail all the things I like about you so that people have no doubt that I'm here of my own free will."

"A press conference is unnecessary," he said, his throat feeling tight all of a sudden. "But I wouldn't mind hearing your list."

She looked away from him, her cheeks turning pink. He liked that—in spite of everything they had done—she still blushed like an innocent. "I'm not sure it would be good for your ego."

"What ego? I'm a terribly scarred man who has lived the past three years in total darkness. It could do with a little bit of boosting. Especially considering the general hideousness of my visage is the topic of conversation around the world."

"Fine," she said, looking down into her coffee. "I would tell them how much I liked the fact that you seem to enjoy it when I talk back to you. That whatever we have between us, you've never made me feel I had to earn it. That for some reason, around you I'm able to be more myself than I've ever been with anyone. Ever. I've spent most of my life trying to behave, trying to be a good person. And being here with you, there was so much freedom to just…not do that." Her blue eyes met his, a strange smile on her lips. "I know that sounds weird. But, I was your prisoner, so I was hardly going to behave in a manner designed to impress you. It was like all of that just faded away. My concerns about being seen as... I don't know."

She blinked rapidly, then cleared her throat and continued. "I thought that passion was the enemy, but it isn't. I had to blame something. When your own mother doesn't want you, you have to find a reason. And then, you have to take that and... make it a lesson, I guess. I had to find a purpose behind what I had been through. The fact that my mother abandoned me, gave me away... and I bound it all up in this idea that giving in to what you wanted could only ever be selfish. But instead of fixing anything I just lost pieces of myself. And with you, I found them. So that's why I'm here. I guess it's not exactly the story the media is looking for, since it doesn't involve a lot of drama and emotional manipulation. But it's the truth."

There was a deep, intense truth in her words that resonated inside him. That he recognized.

That reminded him of pieces that had been lost over the years, that he had found only with her. But, he didn't say anything about it.

"And here I thought it had something to do with my magic hands," he said instead, doing his best to smile at her. Smiling. It was a foreign facial expression now. Lost in all that time spent by himself. And yet, he often wanted to do it for her. To show her that she made him feel something.

"They certainly help," she said, a smile tugging at the edge of her own lips. "I would tell them about that too. You know that's what I meant, don't you?" She stood slowly from her chair, making her way toward him. She leaned forward, putting her hands on his thighs. "When I said that Prince Charming was underrated? I would much rather have a man like you. Suave and sophisticated...it doesn't appeal to me. Not in certain rooms, anyway."

He reached up, pressing his palm against her cheek. "You're very bold for a woman who was only recently a virgin."

"I think I always was. But I hid it. And now

that I'm not hiding it anymore, I really can't bring myself to hold it back at all."

He moved his hand around to the back of her head, curling his fingers into a fist and holding her fast. "Tell me more."

Her smile turned slightly wicked. "I like the way you hold me. Like this. Like you're never going to let me go."

"A man is tempted to believe that you rather enjoyed being taken prisoner, Belle," he said.

"I suppose I did. I was freer as your prisoner than I ever was before."

His certainty faltered. It was a strange thing to say, and while he would like for it to be true, while he would like it all to make sense, he was afraid that if it did…it was perhaps more along the lines of what the newspapers were shrieking about than any kind of organic emotion.

He released her then, unease stealing over him. But, before he could let it take over completely, he reached into his pants pocket and pulled out the small velvet box that had been in there since he got up this morning. "I have something for you," he said, placing it on the table.

She made no move toward it; instead, she stared at him with a confused expression on her face. "What is it?"

"Don't you want to open it?"

"If it's what I think it is, I think perhaps you should open it."

He had not intended on proposing to her. They were already engaged, so he didn't quite see the point to it. Also, he had done this once before. It seemed strange to do it again. With a different woman. Not because he was still so deeply in love with his late wife. He had loved her; he always would. But, it had been a love based on practicality, one that had grown to be romantic over time and with the addition of marriage vows. They'd made a commitment, and he had been happy to make it.

No, that wasn't what gave him pause. Any sort of feeling that he was repeating the past didn't sit well with him. Not when he could never revisit that place. Didn't want to. He was not the same man who had put a ring on Ianthe's finger all those years ago. And he didn't want to begin this as he had begun that engagement in the past.

Still, she wanted this. And she asked for little enough that it would be cruel of him to deny her. He reached out, pressing his fingers against the top of the box.

"I have done this once before," he said slowly. "At a ball. If you were curious. I was wearing a tuxedo, not jeans as I am now. And, she was in a ball gown, not a simple dress. There were people all around, rather than the solitude. She knew it was coming. And I got down on one knee. She was the expected choice for me, and I was perfectly happy to make that choice. I felt a great deal of affection for her, and that affection grew into love. My life had been charmed up until then. As had hers. I had never been denied anything I had ever wanted, and I had never lost anything."

He tapped his finger on the top of the box, then continued. "In the years since that moment, both my parents have passed away. And then, only a year later I lost my wife, my unborn son. All of my hopes for the future. Whatever I thought it might look like, it was all changed in that instant. And so was I. I'm telling you all this because I want you to know I do not expect our marriage to be what my first marriage was. It cannot be. Because I am not the same man. But when I promise myself to you, I want you to know it is with the full weight of knowledge of what can be gained in this life, and what can be lost." He slid out of his chair, getting down on both of his knees, not one, because that seemed a silly gesture for a man of his age, a man of his cynicism. This seemed fitting for a man about to make a vow. "I want you to be my wife. To stand with me as I move forward into this new phase of my life, this new era for my country. It will not be easy. Speculation will always exist. And I am still me, and we both know there is nothing easy about that. But I will be faithful to you. And I will pledge my loyalty to you. To our children. I swear to protect you."

That promise was like granite, because he had failed to protect a wife and child once before. But how could he promise less to Belle now? Even knowing just how human he was. How likely he was to fail.

Still, it sat like ice in his stomach, recriminations coming at him from every which way. How dare he make this promise when he had failed so badly before? How dare he put all this on a woman he had forced into his life, into his darkness?

How dare he try to capture this light, when he had nothing to give in return?

Still, in spite of all that, he opened up the box, revealing a large blue stone he had chosen because it reminded him of her eyes. He didn't tell her that. He said nothing as he wordlessly took the piece of jewelry from the box and slid it onto the third finger of her left hand. "Be my wife," he said, a command more than a question, "and I will be your husband."

"Yes," she said simply, her tone steady, never wavering. "And next time I talk to my father, this is what I'll tell him. That when you asked, I said yes. And that I never once wished I had given a different answer."

She might. Someday, inevitably, she would. But he said nothing about that either, and instead rose up onto his feet and claimed her mouth with a kiss. He deserved none of this. But it was being offered to him, and he could do nothing but grab hold of it.

Belle looked at the ring on her left hand for probably the millionth time since Adam had put it on her finger yesterday. It was…it was both surreal and perfectly real all at once. She could feel the weight of it. And not just of the gem, but all the words he had said when he had placed it on her finger.

She felt…well, she supposed she didn't feel the way a lot of women might about the proposal. She was glad that he had brought up his first proposal, his first marriage. She was glad that he was sharing those things with her, because in a great many ways he kept her separate from the deepest parts of himself. From his past.

It was unspoken, but she still wasn't allowed in his part of the palace. Sure, he spent less time there than he once had, opting to spend his nights in her room instead of in his quarters. But she wanted…she longed to share his bed. Not just hers. She didn't know why it felt essential, only that it did.

She rubbed her chest, trying to ease the ache of her heart. She knew why. She knew exactly why; she just didn't want to dwell on it. It had to do with loving him. And when she had told him all the things, all the reasons why she was with him, she had left that out yet again.

She felt like a hypocrite. Waxing rhapsodic about how brave she was with him, how free she was to be herself. When in reality she was hiding one of the biggest parts of herself. When she had first come to his palace she'd had nothing to lose by being herself with him. And, again, when she had imagined their association had a definite end date, it had been easy for her to throw herself into an affair with him, not worrying about the future. About what he might think of her. As long as he had wanted her in the moment, nothing else had mattered.

But, it was more than that now. Now, it was forever. And so, she was back to behaving the way she always had. Hiding little bits and pieces of herself, holding back anything that felt a bit too raw, a bit too close to her heart.

Suddenly, with the blinding moment of clarity—sitting there in the library that Adam had told her she could use as her own—with the sun sinking down behind the mountains, she realized that all this was about protecting herself, not anyone around her.

She wasn't afraid of passion because of what it might make her. No, she was afraid of passion because of how it might hurt when it was over. Because the rejection from her mother had wounded her so deeply, so profoundly, she had never wanted to be subjected to such a thing ever again.

And so, when it had been only passion with Adam, it had been easy to show him. But now it was more than that. Now it was love. It was all of her, and she was so profoundly afraid that he would reject it that she had gone into hiding once more.

She stood up, placing her book down on the side table by the chair, rubbing her eyes, which were growing fatigued in the dim light. Then she looked back at the ring on her hand. "Adam." She whispered his name, brushing her fingertips over the jewel.

Such a strange thing that this man had captured her so completely. Body and soul. That he made her want to risk things she had kept safe and locked tight for years.

She wanted to give him everything. But, that meant being brave. That meant risking herself. Well, all that was what had gotten her here in the first place. That uncharacteristic showing of bravery that had carried her from California to Olympios in the first place.

She took a deep breath and picked up her phone, scrolling until she found Adam's number—the phone was particularly handy here in the palace, where simply wandering around and finding somebody was about as difficult as searching for someone in a small city—and sent a text.

I'm in your room.

It was a risk. But it was one she was willing to take. She wanted to join all the pieces of herself together, the little fragments she had kept separate, kept buried in order to best protect herself. And to do that, she was going to have to force Adam to do the same. They could no longer compartmentalize their existence. There could be no lines, no walls and no wings of palaces between them.

She took a deep breath and walked out of the library, heading toward that forbidden, protected part of the palace.

This would go one of two ways. Either Adam would send her back to her room. Or, he would open up those forbidden, protected places inside of himself.

She truly hoped it was the latter. But she had no confidence in that.

All she had was hope. So right now, it would have to be enough.

I'm in your room.

When the text had appeared on Adam's phone, he had been in his office seeing to some administrative work. He had not expected to hear from Belle, since she had informed him she was reading a book, and he knew that meant she wouldn't be ready to go to bed for hours.

But the timing of the text was less surprising than the contents. His room. She never went to his room, and he never invited her. She had not gone into that wing of the palace since she had discovered the photograph of him and Ianthe. That had been fine with him. In her room, there was no baggage, the ghosts of the past didn't loom quite so large overhead and the darkness didn't feel quite so impenetrable.

But for some reason, she had now crossed that invisible line, and it was clear she expected him to come and drag her back over it.

He gritted his teeth, standing from his desk and striding from his office. He moved down the hall quickly, his footsteps echoing in the empty corridors. His heart was thundering, hard, restless adrenaline pumping through his veins. Need, anger and a simple, driving force to see her standing there pushed him on. He had no idea what he was feeling because he felt everything. It made it impossible to zero in on one thing. To make sense of any of it.

He made his way down to the end of the hall, passing the sitting area he had found her in last time, and going straight for his bedchamber. One thing had become abundantly clear on his journey from his office. He needed her. He couldn't wait to have her. Even if it would be trespassing on sacred ground to do so, or, perhaps most especially because it would be. He felt sick. With longing, with anger, with a desire that had captured him and taken him over completely. Until he couldn't breathe, couldn't think.

He pressed his palms against the double doors and pushed them open.

Belle gasped, then turned to face him, her eyes wide, her expression that of a deer caught in the headlights of a car.

She was standing in front of his bed. A bed he had shared with his wife. This room that he had shared with his wife. It was still so heavy with memory, with the past. With guilt.

The fact he had allowed himself to sleep elsewhere over the past week had been something of a luxury. Normally, he forced himself to stay here. To linger in it. For his sins, it was a small price to pay.

"What are you doing here?" he asked, his voice deceptively soft.

"I… I thought it was time," she said simply. "Don't you?"

He began to pace the length of the room. "It will never be time. There is never a time for this."

"You have to let me in sometime," she said, and he knew she didn't mean just into the room. "Otherwise, I think our marriage is going to be a lonely one."

"This was our room," he said.

She nodded slowly, then swallowed hard, visibly. "I know. And I'm not… I know… I don't want to replace her. Like you said, this isn't the same. We are not the same, and I understand that. I respect it. Everything you've lost matters to me. I know you might not believe this, and I don't know if you want to hear it, or if it even helps. But in a way I care for her too, even though I didn't know her. Because you did. Because you do. Because losing her hurt you, because you loved her, and the destruction of that has made you the man you are."

She had no idea. She didn't understand. And he didn't want to help her. Because he simply couldn't…he couldn't share it. And more than that, he couldn't stand changing the way she looked at him.

"I just don't want to be locked out," she said. "I don't want there to be vast spaces closed off to me because of the pain in them. You can share it with me. I will never tell you not to feel it."

He knew that she wasn't just talking about rooms in a castle. "Why would you do that? It doesn't make any sense. Why would you want to carry any of this?" He could feel the full weight of his grief just then, his guilt, oppressive, dark and destructive, and he didn't want her to bear any of that. He couldn't stand it if he knew she had been touched by this, tainted by it.

"The usual reasons," she said, her voice small. "I'm only asking you to do this, because I'm going to do it too. Because I'm going to open myself up to you, and I'm going to stop protecting myself. Protecting my pain. You don't have to tell me the same thing. You don't have to feel the same... I just want you. Whatever that may be. However much it may be. And I want that because I love you."

Those words seemed to reverberate in the relative silence of the room. Or maybe they weren't echoing in the room, but inside of him. Loud and endless, and painful.

And he had no response to them. So he did nothing at all, nothing but stand there looking at her as those words sank down inside him, like rain on dry, cracked earth. He had nothing to give back to her, but he let this wash over him, let it fill him, flood him.

She approached him slowly, her hand outstretched. She pressed her palm lightly against his chest, her fingertips skimming over his skin, over his nipples, down his stomach. He took a sharp breath, arousal joining in with that insatiable thing that had absorbed her offer of love for all it was worth.

He responded to her, to her words, to her touch, with every part of himself. His heart was thundering so hard he thought it might burst through his chest, his lungs burning, as though they were too full of air, and yet he could feel himself drowning here above water. And his body...he was so hard he hurt. With his need to press himself against her, join himself to her, in the tight, wet heat of her body. Where everything else was blocked out, all the pain, all the recriminations of the past. When he was inside Belle there was nothing else. He was lost in her, consumed by her, and he needed that badly.

Right now he needed it more than air, and he did not possess the restraint to turn away from that need. She moved closer to him, her hand pressed firmly against his stomach as she leaned in and kissed him, gently at first. Even though it took all the control he possessed he allowed her to guide the kiss, allowed her to dictate how hard and soft it was, allowed her to be the one to instigate invasion.

When her tongue slid along the seam of his mouth he felt a growl resonating inside his chest. He could not be civilized with her, and she had never professed to want it. So, he saw no point in pretending he was anything other than what he was.

That was when his control snapped.

He wrapped his arm around her waist, crushing her to him. He was so very aware of the fact that she was small, delicate and breakable, and that he was testing her limits. But he needed to. He needed to test her against him, against this despair that ravaged him, against the darkness that was always pressing in. Especially here. Never more than here.

Ghosts and regret. Shame and doubt. They loomed large, they loomed dark, oppressive. They were omnipresent, but this was where they lived.

And with Belle's hands on his body, with her lips fused to his, he could feel light inside of him. Could feel a fire burning at the center of his chest, heat and need that blotted out those demons, that darkness, that cold.

It was a small miracle, happening inside him, all around him. She was a miracle.

And she loved him.

A surge of violent emotion assaulted him and

he kissed her harder, walking her back—not to the bed—but to the wall. He flattened his palms against it, on either side of her, his body flush with hers, the hard length of his arousal cradled between the softness of her thighs.

He reached down, grabbed the neckline of that beautiful dress she was wearing and tugged hard. A sharp tearing sound filled the room as the fabric fell away, exposing her breasts. He gazed at her bare skin appreciatively. Hungrily.

"Had I known you were sitting in the library naked beneath your dress I could never have left you alone," he said, each word thick with desire.

"Had I known that," she said, reaching up and touching his face, "I would have made sure to announce it."

He grabbed hold of her wrist, drawing her hand up above her head, pinning it to the wall. Then he reached for her other hand, repeating the same motion, holding her fast with an iron grip.

She arched against him, her breasts brushing against his chest, that soft flesh, the tightened buds of her nipples a sensual assault he had no desire to escape.

With his free hand he reached down, grabbing what remained of her dress and tearing it away. It left her in nothing more than a pair of silk panties that rode low on her hips.

He slipped his fingertip beneath the waistband. Teasing her. Teasing himself. "Did a member of my staff choose these for you?"

"Yes," she said, the word trembling, as her whole body trembled when he continued to slide his finger back and forth, not quite grazing her intimate flesh.

"Somebody deserves an increase in pay. I want to see more." Loosening his hold on her, he moved one hand to her hip and turned her so that she was facing away from him. Then he immediately returned his hold to her wrists, keeping her captive, but this time revealing the elegant line of her spine to his appreciative gaze.

She was bent slightly at the waist, her back arched, her rear thrust out slightly. He curved his hand around to her stomach, sliding it down slowly, then around to her hip until he was cupping her ass.

Her skin was bare, fully revealed by the thong cut of the underwear she had on.

"Exactly what I had hoped for," he said, leaning in slightly, adjusting his grip on her wrists and hip so that he was holding her fast. He arched himself forward, pressing his hardened length to the center of her supple flesh.

She gasped, then made a low, keening sound as he rocked forward harder still, increasing the pressure each time. He slid his hand forward, this time delving completely beneath the silken fabric of her panties to where she was wet with her desire for him.

He pressed the heel of his palm against that sensitized bundle of nerves at the apex of her thighs, then slowly rocked back toward the entrance of her body, sliding his finger slowly into her slick folds, teasing her with the promise of penetration.

She wiggled against him, shuddering out his name, a prayer, a curse. He would take it as both, and happily.

They stayed like that for a while, him pleasuring her with his hand, keeping her pinned against the wall and his body. She rocked her hips in time with his rhythm, arching into his arousal each time she did.

It was hell. And it was heaven. He needed to end it, needed to bury himself inside her, but also, something in him wanted to prolong it for as long as possible. To stay here like this, suspended in limbo, where neither of them was satisfied, where neither of them could ever get enough.

Where the fire burned bright and hot, and he felt like he was standing in the light after so many years in utter darkness.

"Adam," she said, the word ragged. "Adam… please."

He stilled his movements, cupping her sex, keeping the pressure firm. "Please what?"

"I need you. I need you inside me."

A jolt of desire washed through him, and he found himself completely powerless against that simple request. That simple expression of need. He had her pinned against a wall, had her caught between that uncompromising place and his body, rock hard with need for her, and yet, he was the one who had no power. He was the one who felt weak enough to drop to his knees in the face of this blinding need.

With a shaking hand he worked his belt free, undid the closure on his slacks and pushed his pants and underwear midway down his hips. Then he hooked his finger around that insubstantial strip of fabric at the back of her panties and swept it aside.

He groaned at the view before him. The rounded curve of her ass, that sweet, tantalizing view of her feminine flesh between her partly spread thighs.

He could not resist her. He didn't want to. He wanted nothing more than to be buried in her.

He positioned himself at her slick entrance, sliding in just half an inch, testing her readiness, allowing her desire to bathe the head of his arousal.

He swore, grinding his teeth so tightly together he thought for sure he might reduce them to dust.

He grabbed on to her hip again, leaning in with his other hand, pressing her wrists more firmly against the wall, he flexed his hips, drawing her rear back farther as he slid deeper inside her. She gasped, a shiver running down her spine, through her body, and he felt it echoing inside him.

She lowered her head for a moment, and then looked back at him, those blue eyes colliding with his, the electric shot from that unexpected eye contact reaching all the way down to where they were joined, causing him to surge up even more deeply inside her.

He flexed his hips and she groaned; then he withdrew, slamming back into her. He moved his hand around to the front of her body, stimulating her sex with his fingertips as he established a steady rhythm designed to drive them both insane.

She whimpered his name, over and over again, driving him closer, faster than he wanted. He wanted it to go on forever. And like this, it wasn't going to.

He freed her wrists, taking hold of both hips and driving himself hard into her one last time before he withdrew.

"What?" she asked, her tone dazed.

"Trust me," he returned, his voice a stranger's even to his own ears.

He turned her so that she was facing him, claimed her mouth in a deep, hard kiss before taking her into his arms and carrying her to the bed. He set her on the edge of the plush mattress. "Lay back," he commanded.

She complied, her legs dangling over the edge, her head tossed back, her breasts thrust high. She was like a beautiful virgin sacrifice being given to the monster in the manor. And yet, even realizing that, believing it, he would not stop himself.

He was the monster, after all. Past the point of redemption. But if he had a hope of coming close, it would be inside her.

He gripped her thighs, drawing her legs up over his hips, urging her to wrap them around his body. She complied. Then he thrust deep inside her again. She gasped, throwing one arm over her face as he thrust down into her from where he stood at the edge of the bed.

"Adam," she whimpered. "Adam, I need——"

"This," he finished, punctuating the word with a hard thrust. "You need me inside you."

She nodded, reaching up and taking hold of his forearm, drawing her fingertips down to his wrist before moving his hand to her lips. Then she darted her tongue out, sliding along the edge of his finger before sucking it deeply into her mouth. He jerked inside her, the surprising contact nearly pushing him over the edge then and there.

She met his gaze, drawing his hand even closer to her lips, taking a second finger inside and sucking hard.

He jerked his hand back, pressing his palms firmly into the mattress as he gave himself up to the riot of need roaring through him.

He was not considerate. He did not give her pleasure the full weight it deserved. But he could not think of anything else. The demons that always hovered at the edges of this room were tearing at his skin, trying to get past the defenses that had been built up between himself and Belle. With each flex of his hips, every time he drove himself home into the tight heat of her body, he was able to prolong the inevitable. Was able to hold on to that little spark of light she had planted inside his chest.

He held her hard—too hard—and he knew that

he was going to leave bruises behind on her beautiful hips, evidence of how his blunt fingertips had dug into her flesh. He knew that he would leave marks all over her, not just on her skin, but inside her, as well.

He would break her. As he had broken everything.

She loves you, a mocking voice said. *What have you ever done to have a woman love you? And yet, you have earned the love of two different women. And you failed the first one so badly.*

He pushed the thought away, enraged that it had managed to penetrate this moment, that it had managed to get beneath his defenses.

He wrapped his arm around her waist, drawing it down to her lower back, lifting her off the mattress slightly as he moved them both back so that they were fully on the bed. He thrust in, long and slow, pinning them both to the soft surface, pressing her completely beneath his weight. Reveling in the feel of being flush against her soft, perfect form.

He alternated between quick, shallow pulses of

his hips and long, slow glides that took him all the way to the hilt.

She flexed beneath him, meeting him thrust for thrust, her internal muscles beginning to pulse around his length.

She tossed her head from side to side, reaching out and grabbing his shoulders, her fingernails biting into his skin. He hoped that she would leave scars. He hoped that she would make him bleed. He hoped that he would never recover from this. From her. That as much as he would leave an imprint on her body, she would be one on his.

Of all the scars that he bore, he would be proud to bear hers.

It would be the one beautiful mark on his body.

The others were simply signs of failure. Of selfishness. Of the rash behavior of a young husband who knew about nothing but pleasing himself. Who had thought his wife's concerns were silly, and who had prized the comfort of his reputation and of his political alliances more than her comfort.

He had paid. They had all paid. All because of him.

He deserved to look as he did. He deserved all that and more.

What he did not deserve was for Belle to be moving beneath him so sweetly, for her to say his name as she did. For her to love him, when he was more a beast than she would ever know.

But he would take it. Because he did not possess the strength to turn it away, to deny her, to deny himself.

He slammed his hips down hard, his pelvis making contact with that place where she was most needy for him. And he felt the explosion detonate inside her. Her body pulsing around him as she found her release. She lifted her head, sinking her teeth into his shoulder as her orgasm overtook her. And it was that, that primal active possessiveness, that pushed him over the edge too.

On a growl, he gave himself up, spilling himself deep inside her beautiful body, staking his claim in a way he had absolutely no right to.

He deserved nothing, least of all this. But he did not possess the strength to do anything but give himself up to it. To her.

Being marked by her would be the only thing that gave him pleasure, solace, once she was gone.

And he realized, as the remnants of his orgasm washed over him, that he would have to let her go.

The headline didn't matter. Not in comparison with her happiness.

He could not allow her to stay here. He could not allow this woman to stay in this dark, oppressed palace with all these demons simply to gratify himself. He could not allow her to bind herself to him without knowing what he was. And more than anything, he could not allow her to love him. Not him.

Because whether or not he loved her in return didn't matter. Eventually, he would break her. As he broke all things in his life.

The only solution was to allow himself to sink deeper into his own brokenness. Only then would she be safe from him. Only then would he not be a danger to anyone.

He rolled off her, breathing hard, lying on his back and staring up at the ceiling. A ceiling he'd stared at countless nights, replaying his feelings over and over again. Replaying that moment he had reached out to touch Ianthe to find her skin ice cold, to find her already gone before help ever arrived at the accident scene.

Compulsively, he reached out, brushed his fingertips over Belle's cheek. She was living. She was warm, and she was bright.

And unless he let her go, she would not stay that way. Because he knew exactly how this ended. With darkness. With cold.

"You have to leave."

Belle was still catching her breath, trying to orient herself after the force of the climax that had just ripped through her body, leaving her weak and breathless. And then Adam said she had to leave.

"Are we going to sleep in my room?" She had thought for a moment that they had made progress, that he had finally let her in, but, now he wanted to get out of the bedroom. She supposed there were steps to take, and she couldn't be too angry if they were small.

"No," he said, his voice hard. "Not just out of my bedroom. You need to go back to California. You should go back to Tony."

"What are you talking about?" Panic scurried through her like a team of nervous field mice. "I don't want to go. We are engaged. You just gave me a ring."

"You can keep the ring. I don't care. Sell it, if your father needs more money for his treatment."

"I… I don't understand. We made love. We—"

"It was a mistake. All of it. I was being selfish. I was allowing you to sacrifice yourself in order to save my reputation, but I do not require that, Belle. And you should not subject yourself to it."

"I chose it," she protested, "because I love you."

He turned away as though she had slapped him. "You do not love me. Read a headline or two about our relationship, Belle. You have Stockholm syndrome. You have begun to identify with your captor because I cut you off from the outside world so effectively."

"You insulting bastard. How dare you tell me what I feel and don't feel like some amateur pop psychologist? I know my own mind. And I know what I feel."

"Or, you think you do," he bit out.

Rage fired through her. "So, you're going to gaslight me? Tell me how it's actually been so that you can try and deny my feelings?"

"You don't know what you feel."

"Why not? Because I'm a woman, and I'm simply too softheaded to understand my own heart?"

"No," he said, "because you don't know the man that you chose to take to bed. I have never told you the whole story about that night my wife died. I have never let you know why it is I think I'm a monster. You think it's because of these scars?" He sat up, his muscles rippling with the motion. "I don't give a damn about my scars. About the loss of my pretty-boy face. What the hell does any of that matter? I was a monster long before that accident, and all that did was reveal who I actually am. Selfish. Hideous. At least now my face serves as a warning."

"Stop it. Unless you're actually going to back that up with facts I don't want to hear any of it. It's all drama. It's all you running away from something that feels too real for you to handle. You've been hiding for so many years that you've forgotten how to stand in the light."

"No, I know exactly how to stand in the light. In *your* light. And I would steal it, Belle—trust me. Use it all up until you were just as dark as I am."

"Maybe *you* should trust *me*. Maybe you should trust that I'm strong enough to know what I want, to know that I can handle this."

"Do you want to know what kind of husband I am?" He shook his head. "I am selfish. I prized my own reputation, my own happiness above all else. My wife was very pregnant when she died. And she didn't want to go to the gala that evening. No, she wanted to stay home and put her feet up. But I told her in no uncertain terms that it was not to be done. It was important that I be seen there, you see. That I make an appearance, that we make an appearance, because as a couple we were quite the darling in the media. I needed her to come there and look radiant. To look like the happy princess carrying the future of the nation. I wanted to present a specific moment to the media. We were beloved by some of the press, but hounded the rest. Popularity always has two sides. And there were rumors about her, about us, I wanted to dispel. And so, even though she wanted to stay home in bed, I pressed the issue."

"Adam…" She tried to take a breath but she felt oppressed by the pain that was coming off him in waves. It made it difficult to stay sitting up, much less speak. "You can't blame yourself for that. It isn't as though you could have ever known there was going to be an accident. It isn't as though you could have anticipated—"

"It doesn't matter. Of course I couldn't have. I cannot predict the future. And of course I blame the photographer who just *had* to get the photo. Who was determined to try and shove a camera in my poor wife's face, to make more snide comments about her past, about the fact that she was a woman with a certain reputation before she married me, and that I couldn't be certain the child was mine." His expression was fierce. "Of course the child was mine. I knew her. I knew who she was, and that she was faithful to me. But the media was intent on making her into some kind of caricature. Something she was not. I don't blame myself for that. But, I cannot forgive myself for insisting on trotting her out in those circumstances. For not listening to her when she said she was too tired. For not honoring her as I should have done. I loved going out. Being seen. Being part of that glittering world. Why do you think I removed myself from it so effectively after her death?"

She felt as though she had been stabbed in the chest, as though she might begin bleeding out all over the brocade bedspread. Of course, of course he had kept himself locked away. Because he blamed the fact that he liked to go out, the fact that he enjoyed his status. The fact that he had enjoyed that aspect of royal life, and that it had betrayed him. Of course he had punished himself like this. Keeping himself away from people, away from women, away from even his subjects—whom she imagined he loved. He had cut himself off from everything. Everything but this pain. And he had fashioned for himself in this corner of the castle a mausoleum, not to his wife and child, but to his failure.

A monument to his grief and his guilt. She couldn't blame him. Not really. After all, her entire life was a monument to the pain that she felt over her mother's rejection. Her fear of being rejected again. But she didn't blame herself, not really. She never had. Yes, it had made her afraid, but she had always known that the culprit was her mother. That there had been nothing a four-year-old girl could do to make her mother love her more.

But Adam was awash in regret. In what might have been. Adam didn't just have grief, hadn't only experienced loss; he had taken that loss into himself entirely. And he was determined to punish himself forever for it. He was punishing himself now.

He would punish them both, so that he could live in his grief and guilt forever. She thought back to what he had said when they had landed in Santa Milagro. About how part of him wanted to hold that pain, that darkness to his chest forever, to make it matter, to make it mean something.

But it was more than that. He was consigning himself to eternal punishment, eternal damnation. He had played the part of judge, jury and executioner. She wished so much that she could take it all away.

But she couldn't. She knew that without a doubt, sitting there across from him, naked body and soul, that she couldn't take it from him if he didn't want to release it. And living like this... with all these cracks between them, all of these walls, would be the death of her eventually. Oh, not literally. Because whatever the world said about him, whatever he thought about himself, he was not that brand of monster. But emotionally...after all these years of living with so much of herself repressed, she couldn't imagine submitting herself to such a thing again.

To live with a man who was determined to reject the love that she had dug so deep inside of herself to offer him.

But she didn't want to leave him. Part of her wanted to stay forever, regardless of the fact that it would end in her destruction, because at least, if she went down, it would be in a blaze of glory. At least, it would be experiencing the kind of passion she had only ever dreamed of before. The kind of passion she truly hadn't imagined actually existed.

She reached out and put her hand on his shoulder. "I love you," she said again. "And nothing that you can say is going to change that. Nothing that you tell me is going to change that. You think that you're going to uncover some hidden darkness inside of yourself that's going to make me rethink everything?" Her heart felt like it was being squeezed in a vice. "Adam, I have lived my whole life shoving my feelings down, shoving down my desires. I thought I was happy. I thought that the sort of easy moving through life like that was the answer. The answer to happiness, the answer to stability. But it isn't all about *easy*. It isn't all about *happy*. I would rather struggle here with you, deal with this pain, this deep, dark emotion that you feel, fight with you, scream at you, make passionate love with you, than go back home to my safety net. I don't want easy, not anymore. I want real. I want to feel real. I want to *be* real. And I did with you. I do. This is what I want. This crazy, messy thing that we have here. Don't try to protect me from it, because it's the best thing that's ever happened to me. You're the best thing that's ever happened to me."

He shook his head slowly. "I don't want you here. I thought that perhaps it was the answer. I thought that perhaps if I took you to bed here, I could start over, that I could forget. But it isn't only that I can't. I don't want to."

Those words hit their target, lanced her like a sword. She also knew that they weren't right, that they weren't real, that he was protecting himself with them. She could see it, could see it in the despairing look in those dark eyes. He didn't want this, but he was not holding her prisoner; he never had been. He was holding himself captive. And he seemed determined to never allow himself to be released.

She got off the bed, moving to the center of the room, standing there, naked and completely unashamed. "You're going to have to tell me again. If you want me to go, Adam, I'm not going to force myself on you, but you have to look at me and tell me that you want me gone. What happened to you—what happened to your wife and your son—was a tragedy, and you had no control over it. You've lied to yourself, you've taken that guilt onto yourself, and in a lot of ways I understand why. Because you're afraid of being hurt again."

"No," he said, his voice rough. "I'm not afraid of being hurt again. I'm afraid of the damage I can do when I forget who I am and what I am. When I allow myself to fully buy into all that is supposedly good and elevated about me. When I treat myself as though I truly am royal, as though I deserve some sort of greater consideration than those around me. I know how much destruction it can bring. And I will not become that again."

"You're afraid of being hurt again," she persisted, her voice trembling now. "And I don't blame you. My mother isn't dead. She simply rejected me, and I live with that same fear. So I'm standing in front of you now risking that, because I feel like when it comes to love you should do nothing less but risk your whole self, your whole heart. And, I also believe that love is honest. It doesn't just tell you what you want to hear. So, I'm going to tell you the truth. You didn't make the choice to lose her. You would never have chosen to lose your son. But you're choosing to lose me, to lose this, to lose what we could have. Adam, I can never replace her. And maybe…maybe you'll never love me the way you loved her. I don't need that. I just need the best you can give now. I just need you to try. And I need you to choose me. To choose us. Choose life instead of death. You didn't have that choice before. It was an accident. You had no control. But you do now, and you're choosing to kill us. Don't."

She was ready to beg. To get down on her knees. She would; she would do it gladly. Anything to keep him, to keep this. She had no pride where he was concerned, where this was concerned. What good would pride do her?

She had been a child when her mother had sent her away. Packed up her frilly little room that had been more a testament to her mother wanting to appear like a good parent than it had ever been about Belle's taste.

And then she had put her in a town car, bound for her father's house, and told Belle she wouldn't be coming back.

It had broken her. Shattered her world. She had screamed and screamed, determined to make her mother hear her pain, her fear. But her mother had turned away, and so Belle had wept and shouted, all alone in the car except for the poor driver, who was simply following orders. A creature of woe and utter despair.

But she wouldn't dissolve. Not now. Not with him.

And she would be damned if she let Adam do this, if she let him retreat back into the darkness without the full force of her light shining on him. She wasn't afraid to be loud. Not now. She wasn't afraid to love, wasn't afraid to rip her chest open and spill the contents before him.

Because without him, there was no heart to protect. *He* was her heart. He was everything. And she was determined not to lose him. If she did, it wouldn't be for a lack of fighting. Of that she was certain.

"Perhaps you're right," he said, his voice as blank as his expression. He leaned over and flicked on a lamp, the harsh sideways light casting his scars into even sharper relief, the peaks and valleys of his ruined skin looking even more exaggerated now. As though all the darkness, the ugliness, the pain from the inside him was bleeding up through his flesh. "Perhaps I am choosing this. To let you go. But, that is my prerogative. Don't you understand? This is what I want. This is what I am. I am nothing more, and I can give you nothing more. We had fun these past weeks, or at least, something close to what a man such as myself can call fun. I have certainly enjoyed the luxury of escaping into your beautiful body, but it is not love. I've had love," he said, the words choked. "I had love and it's dead. This is not that. And if it is what you want, you should go. It is a kindness that I'm sending you away, Belle, rather than lying to you and telling you what you want to hear. I can keep you here, and I can keep your body for my use, but it is not something that would make you happy. So, if I were you I would retreat gracefully, and with the understanding that I am actually doing you a great service by sending you away."

His words cut deep into her, stabbing into her lungs, making it so she couldn't breathe. And yet, somewhere in the back of her mind, she knew it wasn't the truth. Because of what he said about doing her a kindness. Because, if he were even half as cruel as he was pretending to be now, he would not extend her that kindness. If it was all about sex, all about her body, then he would keep her. Because it would cost him nothing to live. The only reason he was lying was so she would leave.

It hurt. It wounded her down deep. To know he felt that what they shared wasn't love. That it was lesser than what he'd had before, because it was bigger, greater and brighter than anything she had ever had in her life. Than anything she had possibly imagined.

"Do you really want me to go?"

He nodded slowly. "It would be best."

"So you're going to stay here and lick your wounds. And open them over and over again, never letting yourself heal because you're comfortable with this pain and afraid of experiencing any new pain?"

He moved off the bed, so fast that she didn't have any time to react. She backed up against the wall, her movements wild. Adam's hand came up, resting lightly on her throat. "It is not so I don't get hurt again. I do not possess the ability to be wounded any further than I already have been. But if you don't leave, you are destined to be hurt by me. The door is open now, Belle, and it may not be in the future. If I were you I would run. Far and fast. Go back to Tony. Go back to the beach. Go back to your father. He is sick, after all, and perhaps it would be best if you spent what could be his remaining days with him."

His words hit hard, but then, they had been designed to. To wound, to inflict the maximum amount of damage.

And because he knew her so well, better than anyone ever had, they hit their mark unerringly.

She nodded slowly, and he lowered his hand, taking a step back, his expression blank.

"Then I'll go."

She didn't want to. And each step she took matched the rhythm of her heartbeat, a heartbeat that wounded her with each and every pulse. That cut her deep as though the entire organ had transformed into shattered glass.

She didn't want to go. She wanted to stay. She wanted to turn herself around and fling herself at his feet and beg him to allow her to stay. Beg him to allow her to accept the crumbs of his affection.

But she didn't. Not for her pride, because truly, pride had no place in this. She didn't because she knew that if Adam was ever going to realize he could be hurt, if he was ever going to realize that what they had was real, that something in him had changed in the weeks they'd been together…she had to. She had to go in order for him to learn. If there was any chance he might grieve her loss, she had to allow him the opportunity to do so.

But it cost her. Each footstep feeling like a lead weight, each breath like a knife down her throat.

By the time she reached the edge of the corridor, she ran back to her room, not caring if any of the staff members were around to see her distress. When she reached her bedchamber she looked all around, at all the things in the room that had become part of this life that was only borrowed. None of it had ever been hers. Not the clothes, not the sumptuous bed, not the dark, scarred prince that had changed her forever.

She should pack. She should call for a ride to the airport. She should call Athena to bring her a pot of tea and tell her everything would be okay.

She did none of those things. Instead, she took a deep breath, flung herself down face-first onto the bed and wept as though her heart were breaking.

Because it was.

"She's gone. I do hope you're happy."

Adam rolled over in bed, squinting against the light that was flooding his room. He thought for certain he was hallucinating, because it seemed as though Fos was standing in the center of the room, glaring at him with disapproval.

"Who is?"

"Belle," the other man returned. "But then, I imagine that was your goal."

His adviser never came into this part of the palace. All members of staff were forbidden. It was private. It was where Adam kept his pain, and until last night he had never willingly allowed anyone to step inside of it.

For all the good it had done. So, she had left. It was what he had wanted after all. He should feel more triumphant. Instead, he felt nothing but a lead weight in his chest.

"Yes," Adam returned. "I did send her away. It was time."

"She cared for you."

"And if that doesn't show how precarious her sanity is, nothing will."

"Then I suppose mine is, as well," Fos said. "Because for some misguided reason I care about you too. And I care about whether or not you sink beneath the weight of your grief. You had a chance with her. You had a chance to fix some of what was broken. I cannot understand why you would not cling to that for all you're worth. Very few people would have come in here and dedicated themselves to understanding you the way that she did."

"A great many women would love to marry me. I don't have to be handsome. I don't have to be charming. I am royalty, and I can make whatever woman weds me a princess. It's hardly a great feat on my part."

"But you don't need another princess. You need somebody who can see past all that is broken in you. And on a good day, I can barely do that, and I have known you since you were a boy. What you had with Belle…it was the only thing I can see that would ever cast out this darkness. And if you would just stop carrying around so much guilt, you might be able to make room in your arms for love."

Adam laughed, a low, bitter sound. "Love. What has love ever done for me? Absolutely nothing. Nothing but destroy me. And what did I ever give to the woman I loved besides a premature death?"

"Death happens," Fos said. "Life isn't fair. But you are a prince—you are not God. You didn't orchestrate the accident that night. And if you were selfish, then you are no less than human. We are all selfish from time to time. My wife died thirty years ago, and I still remember everything that I did wrong. I still regret so many things, things I would do differently now, that as a young man

I did not possess the capacity to do. But that is life. We cannot hang on to those feelings forever, or how else will we live through the day? You're only a monster because you've decided to be."

He turned to go. "You're finished, I guess?" Adam asked.

Fos sighed heavily. "I might have to be."

On that ambiguous note his adviser left him sitting there in bed as a strange ache began to grow and spread in his chest.

It hurt. It hurt so much, reaching across the bed and finding nothing there. Almost as much as reaching out and feeling his late wife's cold skin.

Suddenly, rage and pain roared through him like a beast and he reached out, grabbing hold of some trinket or other that was on his bedside table. He hurled it across the room. It did nothing to ease the feelings rioting inside him.

He threw his covers off, not caring that he was naked, and stalked down the hall, into the sitting room that often bore the brunt of his rage.

Too much furniture was already destroyed. Already turned over onto its side. He reached up, grabbed a painting of his father from the wall and flung it across the room, feeling somewhat more satisfied when the frame broke, when the canvas bowed. The old man had died and left him too. Why should he leave his painting there to mock him? Like every other thing he had lost. It was too much. It was too much to be expected to endure.

He walked by a chair and kicked it onto its side, stomping heavily on the leg, breaking it in two. So much rage inside him. So much anger. And no one to blame. Nothing to rage at. Ianthe was dead. She was dead, and she was never coming back. His son was gone before he ever had a chance to draw breath. And none of it was fair.

They had both been gone before Adam had a chance to save them. There had never been a chance. The only chance would have been if he simply hadn't gone, but he had, and for all that he was he couldn't go back and remake that decision.

They were his future, they were his heart, and they were gone.

But for some reason, as he thought those words, it was Belle's face that swam before his mind's eye. He pressed his hand against his chest, trying to ease the ache there.

He walked across the room, not caring as he stepped on broken glass, dried flower petals and pieces of furniture. And then he reached the photograph. The one with his wife smiling so radiantly, and with him...with a face he no longer recognized, a light he no longer recognized.

His future and his heart. Three years ago that had been her. It had been her and the child she carried.

But that future, that heart, was for a different man.

Now when he thought of wanting something, when he thought of loving something...it was Belle.

Somehow, she loved the scarred, dark man he had become. She had stood there offering him those things he had thought lost to him forever, and he hadn't even realized it. She was right. She had been right as she had stood there, shouting him down as though she had nothing in the world to fear. He was a coward. A coward who used his grief as a shield, used it to protect himself from ever caring again.

Yes, he had craved those snatches of light that she had given him, but mostly, he had been content to hide in the darkness where nothing could find him. Where nothing could reach him.

And if he stayed here in the darkness, it would certainly offer its own kind of protection. There would be no surprises. Grief, old memories and pain would be a constant. He would be the master of that pain, though. And it would never have the opportunity to master him. It would never sneak up from the depths and shock him, destroy him the way that it once had.

If he stayed here like this, if he stayed alone, he knew exactly how his days would be spent. He knew exactly what he would have stretching out before him. A future full of nothing, a blank endless slate destined never to be filled.

But if he claimed Belle, if he accepted her love, if he admitted to himself that he might love her in return, if he wanted again, hoped again, needed again, then God only knew what the result might be.

Perhaps she would tire of him. Perhaps he would destroy her eventually. Perhaps death might take her, as it had been so cruel to him before. If he cared, if he wanted, if he *needed*, then the future was a bright, riotous unknown filled with hidden patches of darkness and uncertainty.

And if he stayed here—if he stayed like this—this room full of broken memories and dead flowers would be all he ever had.

He bent down, sweeping his fingertips over those dried-out rose petals. How long had they been there?

Years. They had died along with everything else. He hadn't brought any new life into this place since. He picked one up, rubbed it between his thumb and forefinger, grounded into dust. Dust. Death. That was the only thing he had here. Regret, and guilt, and memory.

And she was right. He blamed himself because at least then there was something to be angry at. Because at least then he could make a sick kind of sense of it. And more than that, it allowed him to stay here. To justify never moving forward. To justify this selfish, closed-off existence that was a monument to his wife and son in a way that served no one. Not his country, not their memory and most certainly not his heart.

Fos had spoken of magic spells last week in regard to Belle. And right now Adam felt there might be some truth in their existence. Because standing here, he felt as though he were bound in chains. Chains that were as real as any that could be seen by human eyes. Fos had told him that Belle was the one with the key. The one that possessed the ability to break the bonds. But, Adam had a feeling that wasn't entirely true.

Belle was the reason. But he was the one who would have to do it.

There would be no certainty. No certainty that she would forgive him for the horrible, untrue things he had said to her in his attempt to drive her away. No guarantee that life would continue on smoothly and he would have her until he drew his last breath. All these things required a step taken in faith, taken in bravery and taken in love. The very idea of doing it seemed impossible. Seemed utterly untenable. And yet, he found himself taking a step forward, and then another.

And while he knew very little about the way his life might end up, in the moment he knew exactly what he was walking toward.

It was light. It was pain. It was pleasure. It was love.

It was Belle.

He took his phone out of his pocket, still holding the dead rose petal in his hand. And he dialed Fos's personal phone. "Flowers," he said when the old man picked up. "We need flowers in the palace again."

Between long hours spent in oncology, and then long hours spent caring for her father while he felt ill with the aftereffects of his treatment, Belle felt wrung out and gritty by the time she walked out the back door of their modest home and wrapped a sweater around herself to fortify her body against the sea breeze blowing in off the waves. She walked down the stairs, kicking her shoes off as she reached the sand, making her way down to the water's edge.

If a human could be stale, Belle certainly was. She felt brittle, as though the slightest bit of pressure could break her in half. She felt tired. Broken.

And she couldn't even blame it all on her father's treatments, or the clear physical toll they were taking on him. No, this was all to do with heartbreak. It was all to do with Adam. When she had arrived back home teary-eyed and pale, her father had railed against her monstrous captor with all the strength he had in his frail body. But, Belle had only managed a weak smile, and told him that Adam truly wasn't as awful as he had been made out to be.

Of course her father had protested.

"He took you prisoner over a few photographs!"

"You don't know what he's been through. He's very private. And he's endured so much pain. Just because he was born royal doesn't mean everyone has a right to stare at him, and to dissect his pain."

"You aren't thinking clearly. Obviously he's done something to you during the time you spent with him."

She had nearly laughed at that. "Yes. He stole my heart."

Her father hadn't found that to be a satisfactory answer. What was it with men always trying to tell her what she felt? Always trying to tell her that her feelings were wrong or irrational. She was getting tired of it.

She took a deep breath of the salt air, trying her best to wash herself clean, to let in a little bit of this freshness so that she didn't feel quite so claustrophobic. It was strange what a broken heart did to you. Made everything feel heavier. Even the air.

She looked down at her left hand, at that ring she should have taken off but hadn't yet. She touched it, twisted it around idly as she continued to gaze out at the sea.

Adam. Oh, Adam.

"Belle."

The sound of her father's thin voice carrying toward her on the breeze caused her to turn. And there he was, standing there, leaning against the rail on the deck. And beside him, bathed in the sunlight, stood a taller, more imposing figure.

She looked down at the ring, half-suspicious it

had called him here. Or, more likely that this was a hallucination brought about by her desperation.

"I was going to throw him out," her father said, "but I don't have the strength to handle someone his size on a good day."

"You don't have to do that," she said, feeling dizzy and breathless.

Adam walked past her father without saying a word, heading down the stairs and onto the beach. He paused, kicking off his shoes next to hers. Her father shook his head and walked back into the house, leaving her alone on the beach with Adam.

"You came," she said, her voice trembling. "You really did."

"There is nowhere else on earth for me to go," he said simply, making his way toward her. "There is a place I could stay. I can continue on living in the darkness as I have been. But…it isn't what I want. Not now." His hands were in his pockets, his gaze focused on the ocean be-hind her.

"What did you come here to tell me, Adam? Did you come here to let me know all the other ways I don't measure up to your wife? Did you come here to tell me that you want to take me prisoner again even though you don't have feelings for me?"

He looked at her then, his gaze fierce. "No. Of course not."

"Then I could do with a less dramatic buildup, thanks. Can't you see that I'm here breaking apart? Trying my very best to keep myself together, to keep on breathing, and then you show up. You show up like some...vision out of a dream, that I can hardly believe I'm standing in front of, and you haven't even managed to get to the point of why you're here. It should be the first thing you say. The reason you are here. That should be—"

He cut her off, pulling her into his arms and pressing his mouth to hers. His kiss was urgent, savage, and she reveled in it. Because it called out the savagery in her. Called to that dark, messy place inside her that only Adam had ever reached.

"I love you," he said. "Is that direct enough?"

"Yes," she said, feeling dizzy and breathless. "But you said—"

"Everything you thought about me is the truth. I lied. I lied to us both. I said horrible things, hurtful things, so that you would leave me because I am a coward. Because I thought it best to break my own heart in a way that I could control. When I decided to do it. Not in ten years. Or ten months—depending on how long you could possibly put up with me. Depending on how long it would take for you to finally realize that I'm not a man you love. I'm just a beast that took you captive."

She shook her head. "You're not bad. You're not a beast to…you're…you're everything to me."

"I don't deserve that," he said, his voice rough. "I had sunk so far into my own darkness and I didn't even want to be reached. But you reached out to me when I gave you no reason to, and you started to love me when nothing in me was lovable. I don't understand it, Belle. Because I couldn't understand it, I feared it. And at least buried in the castle by myself I know exactly what's going to happen. If I love nothing, then nothing can be taken from me. And if I blame myself for my wife's death, then it's so much eas-

ier to justify that. To call it recompense instead
of cowardice. But I was hiding. From the world.
And then from you. From my feelings for you.
It isn't that I don't think I can love—it's that I
was enraged because my heart hadn't learned.
Because I can love, deeper and more profoundly
than I ever could because I know how much it
costs. I love you in ways I cannot describe, in
ways that I wasn't capable of loving before I lost
my wife. And all of that seems unfair, it seems
terrifying and it seems like something I would
rather run from than run to, but I can't exist inside of myself knowing that you're out there and
I am there in the darkness. While my light is
here..." He dragged his thumbs across her cheekbones. "I can't stay away from you, even if I
should. I know that I should. For your safety, for
your sake. But I want you too much to do that."
He shook his head. "It could be argued that I perhaps don't love you enough, because that would
mean letting you go, but I can't do that."

"Why do people do that?" she said, thinking
back to what he had said about her earlier, about
respect. "Why do they think if they love some-

one they need to let them go? Maybe, the truth is that if you really love someone, you need to fight through the hard parts, through the fear."

She leaned into him, resting her head on his shoulder. "Maybe you have to love someone enough to accept the fact that it sometimes means pain. That it might mean loss, that it might mean a struggle. That it might mean changing what you're doing and who you are. Sometimes those aren't bad things. Because I know for certain that before I loved you I wasn't whole."

"Belle..."

"I needed to change to have you," she continued as though he hadn't spoken. "And I don't think you're whole without me. So maybe we can dispense with this nonsense that superior love somehow means perfect happiness. I think it should mean passion. I think it should mean struggle, sacrifice, beauty and pain. I think it should mean that I have to open myself up and risk myself for you, and you have to be willing to be heard again for me. You keep telling me that you're darkness. And that I'm your light, but you never once thought that you might be mine?"

"How could that be?" he asked, his voice broken. "It makes no sense."

"I lived a passionless existence. I dated a man for eight months that I didn't even want. I probably would have married him, Adam, secure and happy in the fact that he didn't make me hurt. That he didn't make me ache or want. That I didn't have to risk anything to have him. But you showed me that I could have more—you made me want more. And then you gave it to me. You haven't taken anything from me. You have given me so much more than I could have ever hoped for. The only darkness I've experienced has been those moments without you."

He pulled her into his arms then, kissing her, over and over, deep, fierce and drugging kisses that left her in no doubt of his passion for her.

"You were never my captive," he said, sliding his thumb across her lower lip. "I was only ever yours. From that very first moment I saw you."

"Maybe you're the one with Stockholm syndrome."

He laughed. "Or maybe we just love each other."

She smiled, feeling like light was flooding her soul. "Yes," she said, "I think you're right."

When she had seen him that first day, that day he had told her she would be his prisoner, she had thought him a monster. But it had turned out Prince Adam Katsaros was the man she had always needed.

"I want you to be my wife," he said. "I don't think I have ever said that before. At least not in quite that way. I want you to marry me, be my princess, sleep with me always, give me children. I want it more than I want my next breath."

"I want that too," she said.

"You are my future," he said, drawing his knuckles across her cheek. "You are my heart."

She lifted her hands, tracing the deep lines of his scars that spoke of his pain, that spoke of his strength. Those scars that made him the man she loved.

"And you are mine."

And they lived happily ever after...

* * * * *

MILLS & BOON®
Large Print – October 2017

Sold for the Greek's Heir
Lynne Graham

The Prince's Captive Virgin
Maisey Yates

The Secret Sanchez Heir
Cathy Williams

The Prince's Nine-Month Scandal
Caitlin Crews

Her Sinful Secret
Jane Porter

The Drakon Baby Bargain
Tara Pammi

Xenakis's Convenient Bride
Dani Collins

Her Pregnancy Bombshell
Liz Fielding

Married for His Secret Heir
Jennifer Faye

Behind the Billionaire's Guarded Heart
Leah Ashton

A Marriage Worth Saving
Therese Beharrie

MILLS & BOON®
Large Print – November 2017

The Pregnant Kavakos Bride
Sharon Kendrick

The Billionaire's Secret Princess
Caitlin Crews

Sicilian's Baby of Shame
Carol Marinelli

The Secret Kept from the Greek
Susan Stephens

A Ring to Secure His Crown
Kim Lawrence

Wedding Night with Her Enemy
Melanie Milburne

Salazar's One-Night Heir
Jennifer Hayward

The Mysterious Italian Houseguest
Scarlet Wilson

Bound to Her Greek Billionaire
Rebecca Winters

Their Baby Surprise
Katrina Cudmore

The Marriage of Inconvenience
Nina Singh